this time
Around

THE BENNETT'S BASTARDS SERIES

JENNIE KEW

THIS TIME AROUND

Copyright © 2019 by Jennie Kew
Published by Wooden Key Press
Edited by Hot Tree Editing
Cover design by Mayhem Cover Creations

ISBN: 9780648209454

www.jenniekew.com

"Take my hand, don't be afraid
I'm gonna prove every word I say
I'm advertising love for free
So you can place your ad with me..."

Hard To Handle ~ The Black Crowes

This Time Around – Koru Award 2020 Short Romance –
2nd Place

This Time Around – Stiletto Award 2020 Mid-length
Romance – Finalist

Third Time Lucky – Passionate Plume Award 2019 BDSM
Romance – Finalist

Third Time Lucky – Stiletto Award 2019 Erotic/BDSM
Romance – Finalist

Revenge and Redemption – Sexy Scribbles Award 2018
Contemporary Romance – Finalist

"Be prepared to be taken along on a
wonderful, sexy, heartwarming, sometimes
tear inducing, slightly kinky joy ride!"
Review for *Third Time Lucky*

"The story is heartwarming and empowering.
The plot is gripping and keeps you turning
pages. Definitely one click worthy."
Review for *Third Time Lucky*

"This novel was so romantic! I'm in love, love, love with
Rafe! I will read this book again it was so good!"
Review for *This Time Around*

Prologue

Melville's Cross, May, the worst day of Rafael Bennett's life.

RAFE LEANED back against the bedhead, his long legs stretched out before him and crossed at the ankles, a glass of bourbon in one hand and a boring, long-winded deposition in the other.

He took another swig from the glass, the alcohol burning his throat as he swallowed it down, and tried to focus. He'd been reading the same paragraph for twenty minutes and it still hadn't sunk in.

He was distracted.

Because of *her*.

"'Abby has a new man,' they said. 'We want to fuck with his head,' they said. 'It'll be fun,' they said," Rafe groused under his breath, imitating his brothers and the conversation they'd had the week before. "Fun. Right."

He downed the shot of bourbon.

"Fun" was not a word he had much to do with these days. "Work" was the prominent word in his life now. And "tired". That was a word he definitely associated with. So when the chance came to get out of the city and spend a relaxing weekend with his family, talking shit with his brothers, teasing his sister and sizing up her new man, how could he refuse?

Because at the time he'd agreed to join them, he'd forgotten about *her*.

Jane Melville.

The woman drove him crazy with that mischievous grin of hers, and the way her hips would sway when she walked —towards him or away from him, it didn't matter. She was mesmerising. And dangerous. As beautiful as she was intelligent, and as passionate as she was insane, she had a temper as fiery as her hair and man, could she hold a grudge.

A slow smile spread across his face as he remembered how she'd looked at the town picnic just hours before. So sexy. So enticing. Dressed like the pin-up girls painted on old World War II bombers, licking pink frosting off a cupcake with that talented tongue of hers and staring him down from across the village green, daring him to take action, to take her.

But he hadn't.

He hadn't walked over to her, hadn't driven his hands through her hair, and hadn't pulled her to him and claimed her mouth with all the passion she inspired in him. Instead, he'd avoided her, had kept his hands to himself and behaved like the staid gentleman everyone thought he was.

Everyone except her.

Jane knew him better than that.

Jane knew him better than anyone.

Rafe tossed the document aside and poured another

2

finger of bourbon, sighing quietly as he swirled the rich amber liquid in the glass.

She was getting married soon, and Rafe had rules about that sort of thing. He was a lawyer, well respected in his profession, and most importantly, he was *not* his father.

Ulysses Bennett may have given in to temptation time and time again, dabbling with every other woman who crossed his path, but Rafe was not so foolish. He'd witnessed first-hand the destruction his father's indiscretions had caused, the anguish and the heartbreak. So he'd always vowed to take his relationships seriously.

And he had.

Especially her.

"Is that drink for me?"

Jane's small hand reached out and took the glass, her silky hair trailing over his chest as she leaned up to sip from the tumbler, her naked breasts, small and firm, pressed against his side.

Rafe swallowed hard as he fought to contain the violent emotions welling within him: the excitement and lust he'd felt at finding her in his bed dressed in nothing but a pair of his boxer shorts and silk necktie; his regret, knowing he'd never share another moment like that with her again; and the guilt of sleeping with another man's woman.

Even one as undeserving as Sam Lyndon.

"What are you thinking about?" Jane said, reaching across him to slide the tumbler onto the bedside table.

"You don't want to know."

Sighing heavily, she settled back against his side and twirled her fingertip through his chest hair. "Not this again, Rafe."

"What do you want me to say, Janie?" he said, trying

3

like hell to ignore the tiny zing of electricity he felt everywhere she touched him. "That I'm happy for you?"

"That would be a start."

"Well, I'm not."

Jane swung her leg over Rafe's hips and straddled his body, stared down at him with mischief in her clear green eyes. "I'm getting married, not taking a vow of chastity," she said, emphasising her point by rocking her hips and mashing their bodies together in all the right ways. A moan escaped him and his eyelids fluttered shut.

She felt so good.

He gritted his teeth.

It felt so wrong.

Opening his eyes, he frowned up at her. "Or monogamy, apparently."

Jane shrugged. "Just one of the perks of marrying a swinger," she purred, until he grabbed her hips and ceased her movement. It was either that or flip her over and fuck her again, and Rafe figured they needed to talk more than they needed more orgasms. It was a tough choice to make, but he was sure he'd thank himself for it later. Probably.

Jane's shoulders slumped and her mouth twisted. "What?"

"You know what. Since when are you into swinging? You've always been an adventurous lover, but swinging? Really?"

She folded her arms over her perky tits. "I'm a late bloomer. What of it?"

"You're not a late bloomer, Jane. You're being led by the nose."

"Meaning you think Sam is taking advantage of me."

"Yes, I do. I also hear you've given him access to your

bank accounts," he said, his hard gaze boring into her increasingly pissed off one. "Please tell me *that's* not true?"

"Who told you that?" she demanded, staring at him, her emerald eyes narrowing further and she anchored her hands to her hips. "Exactly how stupid do you think I am?"

Rafe frowned at the question. "What?"

Jane slid from his lap and proceeded to dress. "I'm not some innocent little girl anymore, Rafe, so easily swayed by a handsome face and pretty words. And whom I give access to my money *and* my body is none of your business."

The bottom fell out of Rafe's gut and he felt as though she'd slapped him, her words stinging his raw nerves. None of his business? Jane Melville was none of his—

His chest constricted as raw pain radiated outwards from his heart.

And what did she mean by an innocent girl easily swayed? Was that truly what she thought of their past?

He sat heavily on the edge of the bed, incredulous anger bubbling beneath his skin. "Is that why you've been punishing me all these years? Because you think I tricked you out of your virginity with a come-hither smile and my witty charm?"

It certainly wasn't how he remembered it.

"I don't appreciate the sarcasm," Jane said, her eyes glowing green fire.

"And I don't appreciate the accusation," Rafe fired back. He ran his hands through his hair, then laughed in disbelief and shook his head. "For fuck's sake, Janie, you're smarter than this. Our past aside, you've known Sam Lyndon for less than six months, and I don't know how the hell he's managed to dig his claws in so deep in such a short amount of time, but I can tell you one thing."

"Oh, and what's that?"

"He's taking you for a ride, and what's worse is you're letting him. He's not a swinger, Jane, he's a swinging dick. He fucks every woman who crosses his path and doesn't spare them or you a second thought as he does it. It is completely beyond me how you can even think of marrying that fuckwit when he has zero respect for you."

"That is not true!" she snapped, jabbing a finger at him. "And at least he wants to be with me. You couldn't get far enough away from me."

Rafe was on his feet in an instant, towering over her. "So, what? You're marrying him to get back at me?"

The look she threw at him then made him feel as stupid as he'd just sounded. "Wow. Ego much? Oddly enough, Rafael, my entire life doesn't revolve around you."

"That's not what I meant. I just—" He blew a slow breath out through his teeth then fixed his gaze on hers. "You will never be happy with that prick."

Jane shook her head. "I shouldn't have come here. I don't know what I was thinking," she muttered. Then she stopped and looked up at him, a frown pulling at her delicate features. "And how the hell was I punishing *you*?"

"You know exactly what I'm talking about, Jane." She pursed her lips and shook her head, defiant to the end. Fine. He'd spell it out for her, then. "Every time you break up with someone, you rock up on *my* doorstep, knowing full well I won't turn you away. Why? Why is it *my* shoulder you want to cry on, *my* bed you want to sleep in?"

"I recall you showing up on my doorstep a time or two as well, you know."

"And yet you were still the first one out the door come morning." He shoved his fingers through his hair. "I left you once, and only because I had no choice. You've left me so many times I've lost count. I'm done, Jane. I can't—*won't*—be your whipping boy anymore."

Jane's mouth flapped open, but for once she was silent. Rafe would have laughed had the situation not been so damned depressing.

He'd loved this woman once. Adored her. Worshipped her. Now all he felt in her presence was pain and loneliness. It was his own fault. He should have put an end to their trysts a long time ago, should have moved on, but—

No. No buts.

It was time to let her go.

He reached around her to unlock the bedroom door, then turned away to refill his glass. The door slammed shut as he slammed down the bourbon, the burn of the alcohol all too familiar on this disaster of a day.

Pouring another shot, he sighed quietly. "Goodbye, Janie."

Chapter One

Melville's Cross, August, the second-worst day of Jane Melville's life.

"JANE, put the fork down and step away from the cake."

Jane Melville glared at her best friend over the top of her not-wedding cake, silently daring her almost-maid-of-honour to try something foolish—like pry the triple-layer coconut cake from her cold, spinsterly hands.

The cake she'd worked on for the better part of two days.

It was a freaking culinary masterpiece.

And a colossal waste of fucking time.

She shoved another forkful in her mouth then pointed the utensil at the other woman.

"Back off, Bennett. It's my non-reception, and I'll pig out if I want to," she said around the fluffy, coconutty goodness dissolving on her tongue. "Besides, I'm eating for two."

Abby *tsked* and rolled her eyes. "Yes, I'm sure gorging

yourself on an entire wedding cake is exactly what the baby needs."

"What would you know?"

If the stiffening of her best friend's shoulders wasn't enough to chastise her for such an insensitive comment, her quiet gasp and wide eyes were.

"I'm going to pretend you didn't say that," Abby said, smoothing the distraught look from her lovely face. But her words were stilted, her voice brittle as she absently smoothed her hand over her belly.

Abby couldn't have kids, a point of contention that had contributed to her divorce several years before, and a constant source of heartache for the tender-hearted woman. Although, Jane had to admit, Abby was dealing with it much better these days. Now she had someone in her life who loved her unconditionally.

Unlike me.

Abandoned by her appetite, Jane pushed the cake away. "I'm sorry, Abbs. I didn't mean it like that."

Gracious as always, her friend laid a hand over hers and squeezed her fingers. "I know," she said, then grinned. "But I'm still taking the cake."

Jane snorted, her lips twitching into a short-lived smirk.

Watching as Abby removed the bride and groom from the top of the cake and hacked it to pieces, an air of detachment settled over her. It was no longer her wedding cake, just a pretty mess of flour and sugar and coconut cream.

Still, the thought that the hundred or so guests milling about inside the town hall were about to shove it down their gullets made her sick. It was bad enough they were still out there eating her food and delighting in her misery, just waiting for her to make an appearance so they could look down their noses at her. Pity her.

Vultures.

Well, let them eat her not-wedding cake.

I hope they choke on it.

The kitchen door swung open as the waitstaff came and went, their polished silver platters laden with food and drink, and every time it opened, snippets of murmured conversations drifted through the doorway.

Jane strained to hear them but couldn't make out what was being said, which she conceded was probably for the best. The last thing she needed was to go postal because some old biddy couldn't keep her opinions to herself.

She could already see the headline of tomorrow's daily news: *Jane Melville stranded at the altar, pregnant and penniless.* She figured that was probably better than: *Jane Melville burns town hall to the ground with wedding guests inside, teaching gossips a lesson they'll never forget.*

Blowing out a frustrated breath, she knew the stories would start sooner or later with the whys and the hows and the wherefores. In a town as small as Melville's Cross, good gossip was better than sex.

Not that any of them would know good sex if it jumped up and spanked their arse.

And while being the great-great-granddaughter of the town's founding father afforded her some protection from the poisonous clothesline prattle, she knew better than to hope it would shield her completely.

Or for long.

She was off to a good start though, what with Abby whisking her away from the sudden glare of infamy in the church to the relative safety of the kitchen in the hall before too many people figured out what was going on.

With its single point of entry and limited space, it was easy to keep the looky-loos out in the main hall where they belonged. Of course, having two of Abby's enormous brothers standing guard at the kitchen door didn't hurt.

No one fucked with the twins.

Jane smiled as she remembered watching the whole Bennett clan—her second family—arrive for the ceremony. Well, almost all of them. Henry, Sally, Paul, Sophie, Crispin, Avery, Tobias, Charlie and his modern family, Oliver and his current arm candy, and Abby's fiancé, Wolf. Hell, even Ulysses Bennett had made an appearance. The only one missing was...

Rafe.

She wasn't sure what she thought would happen between them after their falling out back in May, but she'd hoped he'd still be at her wedding. A fool's dream perhaps, considering how adept he'd been at avoiding her every attempt to contact him over the last few weeks.

And she still wasn't sure how she felt about *that* little fly in her ointment.

With a heavy sigh, Jane picked up the tiny bride from where it lay on the table and stared at it, comparing its slender waist and slinky white gown to her slightly distended belly and the loose-fitting lacy number she'd picked up at a second-hand shop.

After all the time she'd spent dragging Abby from one bridal boutique to the next, trying on gown after gown and always leaving disappointed, she'd begun to despair at never finding the perfect dress and had resigned herself to walking down the aisle naked.

It was only while hunting through an op-shop for a completely unrelated item that she'd stumbled upon the dress she now wore. Standing in the dressing room, staring at herself in the mirror, she'd just known: *I'm getting married in this dress.*

But apparently not.

With a wave of disgust—or possibly morning sickness—she tossed the tiny plastic bride aside and picked up the groom, glaring at his smug little face and wishing it was the real thing so she could slap him senseless and scream at him and kick him in the balls with her very pointy bridal shoes.

I'm such an idiot.

And after all her arguing with Rafe to the contrary, apparently she *was* still a sucker for a handsome face and pretty words.

Sam Lyndon had conned her good.

As she'd waited for the groom to arrive, excited and anxious to begin her new life, he'd been emptying out her bank accounts and boarding a plane to God knew where.

And how did she know that?

Because Rachel, the bimbo he'd run off with, had the audacity to send her a text message explaining the situation in no uncertain terms. Oh! And a photo of her holding two boarding passes while sucking Sam's cock. And Jane knew it was Sam's cock. The strawberry-coloured birthmark on his junk was a dead giveaway.

But just as she began silently wishing the cabin pressure in the aeroplane would make Rachel's fake boobs explode, something shiny caught her eye.

A minute later, Abby sniffed the air around her. "What is that smell?"

Jane snapped shut the lighter in her right hand and stared at the small plastic groom in her left, smirking at the blistering hole where his genitals used to be.

"Give me that!" Abby said, snatching the lighter out of her hand.

Jane shrugged, unrepentant. "What? You took my cake away."

Her friend sighed and slowly shook her head, but there was no real censure in her expression. More an indulgent acceptance that she was stuck with the crazy lady in the wedding dress as her best friend forever. "Come on. We'll take you home."

"We?"

Wolf appeared behind Abby and draped his suit jacket around her bare shoulders. "It's getting chilly out," he said, pressing a kiss to her temple. Then he lowered his mouth to her ear and said something that made her smile.

Jane wanted to grin at them like she usually did, to bask in the heat of their adoration for one another and celebrate their happiness for the miracle it was. Ordinarily she was their most enthusiastic cheerleader, but now her lips were frozen in a permanent flatline.

She had nothing left to give.

Not today.

So she just stared at them, watching as Wolf stroked Abby's cheek with the blade of his finger, one corner of her mouth lifting at whatever he was murmuring in her ear.

And Jane simply felt... cold.

So cold.

And not from the chill in the air, either. No, this chill came from inside her, deep down in the dark place she tried so hard to hide from the world. The place that held all her darkest memories and unfulfilled desires and all the broken pieces of herself that she'd never figured out what to do with or how to fix.

Thirty-two years of shit just swirling around in the pit of her soul, draining every ounce of happiness out of her.

Usually it was easy for her to keep it all locked away, like a monster in the basement.

Usually.

Unable to look at her friends any longer, she turned away. "Let's go."

Shoving the kitchen door open so she could peek outside, she spied the Bennett twins still standing guard. Both of them watched her as she stepped into the hallway.

"How're you feeling, sweet pea?"

Toby's nickname for her had always made her smile, made her feel like she really was one of the family, but today... *nothing*.

She felt nothing.

Apathy shrouded her every move, every thought.

She did hear something though. "Let me through, you walking man-bun."

"Make me, you pompous arsehole."

"Let me see my sister."

"She's more my sister than yours, dickwad."

Peering between the wall of muscle that was Toby and Charlie Bennett, Jane saw their younger brother, Oliver, arguing with her older brother, Richard.

She reached up and tapped Charlie's shoulder. "Let him through," she said quietly.

"Ollie, stand down," Charlie said, then stepped aside to let Richard through.

Taking her hand, he led her away from the Bennetts. "I appreciate them taking care of you and all, but for fuck's sake, Janie, they're not the only ones worried about you." He shoved his hand through his hair, and she noticed how dishevelled the usually immaculately groomed Dr Richard Melville looked. "How are you feeling? Do you need anything?"

Not giving herself time to ponder his concern, she shook her head. "Abby and Wolf are taking me home now."

"Oh. Okay." He took his jacket off and gave it to her.

"Put this on. There's a storm coming in over the mountains. It'll be cold outside."

Sliding her arms into the sleeves of Richard's jacket made her feel so small, like she was a kid again playing dress-up in their parents' clothes. She wrapped the jacket around her, absorbed his body heat. "Thank you," she said, her voice flat, lifeless.

"Have you spoken to Scott Turner yet?"

Jane nodded. "The good sergeant popped by a little while ago. Wants me to see him tomorrow morning to file a report."

"Good." Suddenly her brother pulled her into his arms and hugged her tightly. "I know I'm pretty crap at being a big brother, Jane, but I do love you, and you don't deserve what Sam did to you today. You know that, right?"

"I know," she said, the sting of tears making their presence known. "And I love you too." When she pulled back, she added, "Can you stay and help Mum and Dad clean up the hall? And someone needs to check on the rental car and—"

"Consider it done," Richard said, and then he smiled. "Now, I want you to go home, take a long, hot bath, have a good cry, and eat a shitload of junk food. Doctor's orders, okay?"

A tiny smile managed to lift her lips for just a moment, and she threw her arms around him again. "Whatever you say, Doc."

The house was dark when Jane entered, the overcast sky blocking the afternoon sun and casting everything into shadow.

It suited her mood. But three seconds later, Abby followed her inside and down the hall, flicking on every light switch as she went.

Mood killer.

And what was up with Richard being so... *nice?*

Usually he was a selfish, entitled pain in her arse. But today.... Jane snorted, thinking she must *really* look like shit if Richard was taking pity on her.

Abby called out from down the hall. "Jane? Do you want me to run you a bath?"

Slipping her brother's jacket off and tossing it over the back of a chair, Jane followed her friend's voice and joined her in the bathroom.

"No thanks. I just need help getting out of this damn dress." She kicked off her shoes.

"Do you want me to stay with you tonight?"

Shaking her head, she said, "No, I'll be fine." Then she looked over her shoulder to where Abby was painstakingly unbuttoning the wedding dress and forced herself to grin. "Besides, you're only offering so you can get out of clean-up duty at the hall."

"The thought did cross my mind," Abby said before twisting her mouth into a grimace. "Especially since Richard will be there."

"Yeah, he was weird earlier, being all nice to me and shit."

"He's your brother, Jane. He's supposed to be nice to you."

"Yeah, but... I don't know. He seemed... different. Off, ya know? Not his usual cocky self."

A quiet sigh sounded behind her as Abby continued popping buttons. "Laura left him."

Spinning to face her friend, mouth open and eyes wide,

Jane grabbed Abby's forearms. "What? How do you know? And more importantly, why didn't anyone tell *me*?"

"He said he didn't want to take the spotlight away from you on your wedding day."

"Maybe he should have," she grumbled, then turned around so Abby could resume button duty. "Tell me everything."

"Not much to tell, really. He came to see us last night, me and Wolf. He didn't say why Laura left, just that she'd packed up the kids and gone, and then he apologised for the stunt he pulled at your engagement party."

Jane smirked. "Did you apologise for breaking his nose?"

"Fuck no! I was married to your brother for five years, and he cheated on me for three of them. He should be thankful that's all I broke. Still," she said, the humour dropping from her voice, "he seems pretty upset."

"Upset he got caught, perhaps. Probably diddling some nurse at the hospital. Idiot never learns."

"I don't know," Abby said. "He seemed genuinely heartbroken."

Jane repressed an unconvinced snort and kept any further thoughts on the matter to herself. She'd always been the more cynical of the two women, but as much as everyone liked to joke otherwise, she did, in fact, know when to shut up.

A moment later, Abby announced, "There. All one hundred tiny bloody buttons undone."

Jane shimmied out of her wedding dress and handed it to Abby.

"Where do you want me to put it?"

Another wave of nausea hit her and she swallowed back bile. "The rubbish bin seems appropriate."

Abby held up the dress and stared at it for a moment, then said, "How about we take it to The Forge? Come over tomorrow for breakfast. We'll have a ceremonial dress burning and, I don't know, toast marshmallows or something."

The first genuine smile Jane had felt all afternoon spread across her face at the idea of setting fire to the lacy symbol of her demise, but... "I have to go to the police station first thing in the morning."

"Okay, we'll make it lunch instead."

"Deal," she said. "And as we watch it burn, I'll have a ginger beer on the rocks and pretend it's bourbon."

"Mocktails all round," Abby agreed. "Now are you sure you don't want me to stay with you tonight? It's really no trouble."

Jane took Abby's hands in hers and gently squeezed them. They'd been best friends for as long as she could remember, and she loved her like a sister, but all she really wanted was to be left alone.

"Abbs, I'm fine. I mean, let's face it, this marriage was little more than one of convenience anyway. Obviously more convenient for him than for me."

"Yeah, but you still cared for him."

Jane dropped her gaze. "But I didn't love him." She shrugged. "Maybe this is all just karma coming to bite me in the arse."

Abby *tsked*. "There's no such thing."

"Yeah, well, I guess it's a moot point now anyway. And you really should go. Wolf has been waiting for you in the car all this time."

Her friend blushed and flicked some invisible lint from the wedding dress she'd draped over her arm. "Oh, he doesn't mind waiting."

Jane raised one brow in silent question.

A broad smile stretched across Abby's pretty face as she explained, "For every minute I make him wait, he'll add another smack to my next spanking."

"You've been in here for almost twenty minutes," Jane said, eyes wide.

She didn't get off on spanking the way her friend did, couldn't even begin to imagine surrendering that much control to someone. Sure, she enjoyed a firm hand on her arse during sex, relished a tiny bite of pain to push her pleasure higher. But letting your partner smack you until your arse was so red you couldn't sit down, letting them control your orgasms?

No thank you.

Abby, however, sighed happily. "I know."

With a laugh and a shake of her head, Jane pushed her friend towards the door. "Go. Have a good night. One of us should."

A slight frown appeared on her friend's face. "If you change your mind...."

"You'll be the first to know," Jane promised, even crossing her heart as she said so.

Abby yanked her into her arms. "I love you."

Jane returned her friend's embrace. Tightening her arms around the much taller woman, she said, "I love you too." Then she eased up onto her toes and kissed Abby's cheek. "I'll see you tomorrow."

With Abby finally relenting her nanny duties and leaving the house, Jane stripped out of her underwear and climbed into the shower. Then, slapping her hands against the wall, she finally let loose the scream that'd been building from the moment she'd realised she'd been duped.

It erupted from deep inside her, tapped into that well of

shit she kept buried and hidden from the world, and bounced off the bathroom tiles like a pinball. But the sound did nothing to relieve her grief or diffuse her rage.

It did little more than make her throat raw.

Her cloak of apathy well and truly shaken off, Jane's emotions trampled her like a herd of startled elephants. She laughed in disbelief, cried in resolution, screamed again and vowed bloody vengeance. She beat her small fists against the tiles, then scrubbed every inch of her body ten times, the feeling of being unclean sticking to her like a bug on flypaper.

How could I have been so stupid?

She used to scoff at women who fell for smooth-talking conmen and their scams, was always so assured of her intellectual superiority, so certain *she'd* never get caught in their nets.

Yeah, no one had ever accused Jane of being humble.

Bossy, abrasive and conceited, sure, but never humble.

Well look who's choking down a big ol' piece of Humble Pie now!

Tired of working two jobs and finally in a financially secure position, Jane had been so damned eager to branch out on her own, to start her own business.

To prove she was more than just Alec Melville's daughter.

She'd trained at Le Cordon Bleu, for fuck's sake, and she was going to show the world what she could do.

After Christmas she'd attended every culinary business function, industry luncheon and meet-and-greet cocktail hour she could beg, borrow or steal an invitation to, not once entertaining the idea of failure, because for Jane—for a *Melville*—failure wasn't an option.

No, she came from a very long line of overachievers and

knew the value of success, and yet here she stood, her ambition crushed, her bank accounts emptied, her bubble burst.

A failure.

And it was no one's fault but her own.

Never trust a man who promises the moon.

But she'd done it anyway.

Stupid, Jane.

As she stepped from the shower, she clutched her stomach and pressed her hand to her mouth, then dashed to the toilet, arriving just in time to throw up without making a mess on the floor. When her stomach was empty, she slumped in a heap on the tiles and scrunched up her nose, the delightful aftertaste of stomach acid and coconut cake souring her mouth and throat.

"Morning sickness, my arse," she muttered as she struggled back to her feet and rinsed her mouth out. "Morning, mid-morning, afternoon, evening, middle-of-the-fucking-night sickness is more like it."

Staring at her reflection in the bathroom mirror, Jane hardly recognised the stranger looking back at her. With her face clean of make-up, her freckles stood stark against her naturally pale skin, as did the dark circles under her eyes.

She looked as exhausted as she felt.

Standing sideways, she smoothed her hand over her belly. The doctor had said she was around three months along, edging into her second trimester. Due to her naturally slender figure, her stomach was already rounding out, enough to confirm who the father was. His family only did one size.

Big.

Jane had managed to hide her pregnancy for the most part under winter clothes and extra layers, so much so that not even Abby had noticed, but her best friend had known something was up. When she'd finally caved in and told her about the baby, her friend wasn't surprised. A little pissed off Jane hadn't told her sooner, but not surprised.

"Two guesses who the father is," she'd said, one brow raised and lips pursed in a knowing look, practically daring Jane to deny Abby's brother was involved somehow.

She hadn't. "One guess actually. Sam always uses protection."

And Rafael Bennett didn't.

Not with her, anyway.

And wasn't *that* going to be an interesting conversation when it eventually took place?

Sighing quietly, she squeezed the excess water from her hair and felt it trickle down her back, then shivered and clenched as it slipped between her arse cheeks.

"Fuck my life."

Chapter Two

Jane stood in the doorway of her bedroom, cocooned in a fluffy pink dressing gown, her hands a flurry of activity as she dried her hair.

She wasn't going to think about how she was supposed to be boarding an aeroplane to Melbourne, how she was supposed to be starting a new life with her husband and not standing in the middle of her childhood bedroom, dripping water on the floor.

"Arsehole," she spat.

"That's one word for him."

"Jesus!" Clutching at her chest, Jane spun towards the intruder and blew out a lungful of air. "You scared the shit out of me."

A rumble of thunder overhead and a crack of lightning added to the overall creepiness of the situation.

Her bedroom, like the rest of the house, was bathed in shadows from the brewing storm, but she needed to see him. Unable to face the harsh glare of her bedroom light, she switched on her bedside lamp instead.

Its soft glow barely illuminated the room, but it cast

enough light to outline the large ethereal figure occupying her reading chair in the corner.

Rising from the armchair, Rafe ignored the social niceties and said, "Is it true?"

His voice was gruff, deep. *Sensual.*

Great. Juuust great....

As always, his nearness made her shiver with anticipation. It screamed along her veins and arrowed downwards, and she fought the urge to squirm.

Clenching her jaw, she tightened her dressing gown and forced back the intense sexual awareness she'd only ever felt for one man. *Rafael.* And if he was here to add insult to injury, so help her, she would—

"Why?" She snapped out the word. "Did you come to gloat? Say I told you so? Well you can save it. I'm not in the mood for one of your lectures." Rafe moved closer and Jane took a step backwards, almost gasping as he stepped into the light. "You look like shit," she said, lifting her chin in a show of bravado. "Don't you ever shave?"

Large hands settled over her hips and prevented her from retreating farther. Listless blue eyes stared down at her, underscored by dark smudges. He looked like he hadn't slept in weeks. He smelled almost as bad.

Eyes narrowing, she slapped his hands away. "Have you been drinking?"

A contemptuous look flickered over his features, then just as quickly disappeared. "Of course I've been fucking drinking," he growled, his rich voice rasping over her last nerve. Then, like the cold-hearted bastard he was, he just stood there, unmoving except for the gentle rise and fall of his chest.

Unflappable.

Unfeeling.

The only consideration stopping her from kicking him out of the house was the fact he didn't sound anywhere near as drunk as he smelled.

He continued his interrogation. "Answer the damn question."

Tossing her hair towel aside and anchoring her hands on her hips, Jane glared up at him. "Ask me a damn question worth answering."

She felt a moment of triumph when Rafe's mouth tightened into a thin line. A reaction. Small, but not insignificant.

He spoke through gritted teeth. "Is it true? Are you pregnant?"

Unease slid along her veins, but she lifted her chin again, uncertain, scared, but determined and unashamed. "Yes."

He stepped closer, invaded her personal space. "Is it his?"

She knew what was coming. "No."

His voice softened. "Is it mine?" Fathomless blue eyes watched her, intense and... *hopeful?*

Jane was tempted to lie. But she didn't. Couldn't. "Yes."

"You're sure?"

"The timing fits."

His jaw tightened. "How long have you known?"

She mirrored his expression and firmed her voice. "Six weeks."

Rafe closed his eyes and breathed deep, and Jane was tempted to rest her hand on his broad chest, to feel the life, the warmth that radiated off him. To reassure him somehow that everything would be all right.

An absurd thought considering how very *not* all right she was currently feeling.

Stupid hormones.

"Why didn't you tell me?"

She scoffed at the accusation in his voice. "Tell you? I've been trying to tell you since I found out. I've called. I've left messages. I even went to your office and spoke to that horrible assistant of yours. I told her I needed to speak with you urgently, but she said you were in court and would get back to me when it was more convenient. So tell me, Rafe, would now be a good time? Is it *convenient* for you yet?"

To his credit, Rafe's face was a twisted combination of horror and shame. "I didn't think—" He shoved his hands through his hair as he paced back and forth across the room. "I thought—"

"What did you think, Rafael? That if you ignored me for long enough, I'd just give up and go away? That is what you wanted, isn't it? For me to leave you alone once and for all?"

His reply was barely more than a whisper. "Yes."

Jane sat on the foot of the bed, her back ramrod straight, and folded one leg over the other. "Congratulations. Now you get exactly what you wanted. You needn't worry about a thing, Rafe. I don't expect anything from you. You don't even have to acknowledge the kid is yours if you don't want to. In fact, it's probably preferable if you don't."

He visibly straightened, his face twisting with hurt. "What did you say?"

"I was just left at the altar by a conman who used my wedding day as a distraction so he could steal my life savings and fly off into the sunset with another woman. I think I've suffered enough humiliation for one day, don't you? Having the town discover the baby I'm carrying doesn't even belong to the man I was going to marry? No. Just... no."

Rafe shoved his hands through his hair and paced across the room, his agitation as obvious as his distress. "If I'd answered the phone when you called, if I'd known about the baby.... Fuck." He stopped and stared at her, his dark blue eyes clouded by uncertainty. Rafe was never unsure about anything. "Would you have gone through with it? The wedding?"

Jane heard what he wasn't saying. "Depends. Would you have wanted me because you want to be with me or simply because I was pregnant?"

Time seemed to stretch between them as he stared at her, his expression shuttered. Then he exhaled and his body seemed to collapse in on itself, like a deflating balloon. "I don't know."

Jane lifted her chin, proud of herself when she stopped it from wobbling. "Neither do I." Turning away from him to hide the tears silently tracking down her cheeks, she said, "I think I'd like you to go now. Please."

But he didn't.

Instead he came to where she sat on the bed and knelt before her, then gently lifted her leg and spread her knees apart, wide enough for him to nestle between them.

"Rafe, what are you—"

He silenced her with a kiss, soft and gentle but fleeting, and moved his hands to rest on her hips. "Please," he whispered, resting his forehead against hers.

Jane swallowed hard, his nearness, his pained voice tugging at her heartstrings. Not trusting herself to speak out loud, she merely nodded.

Slipping the knot at her waist free, Rafe pulled the tie undone and slowly opened her dressing gown, revealing her naked body.

Cool air rushed in, chilling her damp skin. Her nipples stiffened to hard little peaks and her breasts tightened.

Rafe's breathing staggered, and despite everything, Jane smiled. His reaction to seeing her naked had never wavered, no matter how much time or how many bitter words passed between them.

From the moment they'd first declared their love for one another, he'd never hidden from her how much he desired her. How much she affected him.

It was nice to know some things never changed.

"So beautiful," he whispered, trailing his fingertips down her side, skirting the edge of her small breasts and making her shiver more than the cool air ever could. But when he reached her stomach, his touch grew hesitant.

Like a bomb disposal expert.

"It won't explode," she murmured.

He snorted and his body shook for a moment before he shut down his laughter.

Tentative fingers spread across her stomach. To the untrained eye, she merely looked like she'd eaten a large meal, the slight bulge of her waistline barely noticeable. But as Rafe's fingers stroked back and forth against the hard lump of her belly, it finally hit home.

Jane was *pregnant*.

Of course, she'd known she was pregnant for weeks— the endless vomiting made it hard to miss—but between organising the wedding and the move to Melbourne, plus putting together a business plan and the hundred and one day-to-day things she had to take care of, processing her changing state of womanhood kept being pushed further and further to the back of her mind.

But now that she'd been unceremoniously dumped and

robbed blind, her schedule had suddenly cleared right up and she had nothing left to do *except* think about her baby.

Rafe's baby.

Their baby.

Rafe chose that exact moment to press his firm lips against her stomach and whisper, "Hello, little one. I'm your dad."

The tenderness in his voice had tears leaking from Jane's eyes at an exponential rate, and a longing to reach out and run her fingers through his dark silky hair, to cup his cheek in her palm and feel his breath caress the sensitive skin at her wrist.

"I can't wait to meet you." He pressed another kiss to her belly, his lips warm as they lingered on her skin, then sighed softly. "The truth will come out eventually, Jane. You know that. But until it does, I'll keep your secret." Then he rose and turned towards the window, shoving it up as high as it would go and swinging one long leg after the other over the sill. He didn't look at her as he snuck out the way he'd obviously snuck in, and in that deep, sensual voice, he said, "If you need anything, ask."

Then he was gone.

And her tears fell in earnest.

Rafe squinted against the rain as he trudged through town, around the back of the pub, up the hill and through the scrub to Bennett's Road.

It wasn't a shortcut as such, considering the twenty minutes it took to walk home that way as opposed to the five minutes it would have taken by car, but the well-worn bush track that led to The Forge had been used by the Bennetts for decades.

Rafe knew it like the back of his hand.

And a good walk, uphill and facing into the storm that had cracked open the skies five seconds after crawling out Jane's window, was exactly what he needed.

His thigh muscles burned as he made his way up the hill, his boots sinking into the muddy ground and his jeans soaked through. The wet denim clung to his long legs and restricted his movements, and his T-shirt stuck to his skin, but there came a point where he stopped noticing how wet he was and could focus on only one thing.

I'm going to be a father.

At least he hoped he was. Hoped with a desperation he never knew he owned.

But years of listening to people tell lie after lie to avoid the consequences of their actions blended with the anxiety gnawing away inside him, begging him to look at the situation objectively. Yes, there was every possibility Jane's baby was his, but just as much of a chance that it wasn't.

And it was the latter option that had his stomach in knots.

Rafe exited the scrub edging the road, The Forge looming large before him. Crossing the dirt road in front of the house, he jumped over the tiny stream forming in the gutter and a moment later was through the front door, down the hall and standing in the welcoming warmth of the lounge room.

"Your sister will have your guts for garters when she sees the mud you've tracked in here."

Ulysses Bennett stood by the fireplace, warming his weathered hands. A tall, slim man with piercing blue eyes, scruffy silver hair and a neatly trimmed silver beard, his father struck an imposing figure, even at the age of seventy-two.

Recently single, the family patriarch had moved back home. How long he stayed this time depended on how long it took for his next conquest to come along. That coupled with the fact the entire Bennett family was home for Jane's wedding meant the house was overflowing with people. Large, tall, sometimes very loud people.

Not that that was anything new.

The Bennett household had always been a full one, but Rafe had grown used to living by himself in the quiet confines of his city apartment.

By moving home permanently, he'd seemingly given up that solitude, exchanged it for kookaburras laughing outside his window at the butt-crack of dawn and trying in vain to block out the sounds of his sister and future brother-in-law "trying to be quiet" as they went at it hammer and tongs at all hours of the day and night.

I need my own place.

"Last I checked, this was your house, not hers," Rafe said. Even so, he toed off his boots, carried them to the back door and stacked them neatly on Abby's exquisite wrought-iron shoe rack. His sister's skill with the metal rivalled that of his brothers, Oliver and Henry, and they were widely regarded as being at the zenith of the art form.

Turning back the way he came, Rafe saw what his father had and realised the old man was right. Abby would pitch a fit if she saw this mess. With a ragged sigh, he pulled his soggy T-shirt off and used it to clean the floor. His father watched him, amusement etched across his face.

"So," Ulysses said when Rafe joined him by the fire, "is the kid yours?"

His gaze darting to meet his father's, Rafe wondered

exactly how much the old man knew. "How do you know about that?"

"I have nine children," Ulysses said. "You think I don't know what a pregnant woman looks like?"

Rafe swore. "Who else knows?"

"After the fiasco at the church, I think it's safe to say the whole town will know she's pregnant by tomorrow," his father said, scratching his chin. "The fact Sam Lyndon may not be the father? Well, your sister assures me only a handful of people know about that. Of course, that handful includes Mary and Alec."

Rafe closed his eyes and pinched the bridge of his nose. "*Greaaat*," he said, drawing the word out. Jane's parents already hated him, and he could only imagine which level of Hell they were cursing him to this time.

"So, is it?"

Rafe sighed and rubbed the back of his neck. "Jane says it is."

"You think she's lying?"

"No. I think *she* thinks the baby is mine, but...."

"But?" his father urged.

"But that may just be wishful thinking on her part."

Ulysses raised a brow at him. "That seems a tad arrogant. Even for a lawyer."

"Not when you consider her alternatives: an arsehole who left her broke and humiliated, or some random sleazebag she hooked up with at one of those stupid swinger parties the arsehole took her to. Any way you look at it, I'm the more respectable option. Even if I am a Bennett."

Ulysses threw back his head and barked a laugh at the ceiling. "Respectable and Bennett don't usually go hand in hand in this town, my boy."

"Why do you think I left," Rafe grumbled.

"I thought you left to protect the woman you love."

"Same thing. And I don't love Jane," he said, shifting uncomfortably as he did. "Not anymore."

"Uh-huh." His father slid him a sideways glance and watched him. Rafe tried not to fidget—he was a grown man, for fuck's sake—but Ulysses Bennett had a way of making people talk, of breaking down barriers and getting to the truth underneath. It's what made him such an amazing artist.

And a formidable parent.

The Queensland Police should be so lucky to have interrogators as good as his father. "Are you going to tell me what's really bothering you?"

Rafe crouched down to feed more wood to the fire, debating how much to tell the old man. By the time he stood up again, the decision was made. He'd know soon enough anyway. But remembering Jane's insistence on secrecy had Rafe spitting out his next words like poison.

"Jane doesn't want anyone to know I'm the father. Says she's been humiliated enough."

His father shot him a pitying look. "Ouch."

"She'd rather everyone think the father of her baby is a fucking conman than me," he said, throwing his hands in the air.

Ulysses frowned. "What did you say?"

"What *could* I say?" Rafe seethed. "I told her I'd keep her secret. For now."

"And how do you feel about that?"

Bracing his hands against the mantle, Rafe leaned into the rough stone, felt the jagged edges push against his palms and threaten to cut him. He welcomed the pain. "All I feel right now is angry."

"Understandable. But I wouldn't let it fester if I were you. That won't help anyone, least of all Jane and the baby."

Rafe snorted humourlessly.

"What *are* you going to do?" his father pressed.

"I don't know." He sighed. "I know a baby won't just magically fix everything between us."

"No, it won't," his father said, his simple statement heavy with the weight of first-hand knowledge.

Rafe stared into the fire. He'd been that baby once. The one who failed to fix his father's relationship with his mother.

"Christ," he swore, shoving away from the fireplace and running his hands through his hair. "I moved back home because I wanted a quiet, simple life. Why does everything have to be so complicated?"

Making himself comfortable on the couch, Ulysses chuckled. "No one ever said life was easy, Rafe. And if you wanted quiet and simple, you should have stayed the hell away from Jane Melville. Too much like her mother, that one."

"Wait, what?" He raised one dubious brow. "Mary was a hellion?"

Ulysses laughed again. "From the day she was born." He shook his head. "How she ended up married to someone as morose as Alec Melville is completely beyond me."

Good question. "I don't suppose you have any advice you'd like to share?"

His father waved him off. "You don't need an old fuck-up like me telling you what to do. Besides, it doesn't matter what I say. You'll just do what you always do: protect Jane."

With a heavy sigh, Rafe sank into the armchair near the fire and pushed his damp hair out of his eyes. Jane was right.

He needed a haircut. And a shave. "I don't know if I can this time."

"Then you'd better figure it out quick smart. This back and forth you two have going on, this push-and-pull nonsense, it can't continue. Both of you need to grow up and make a decision. You're either in or you're out. With a kid in the mix, there can be no in between. In or out, Rafael. Pick one."

Rafe stared at his feet, dug his toe into the well-worn Persian rug and traced the faded swirls of pattern. "What if the kid isn't mine?" he said quietly. His heart hurt even thinking the sentiment, let alone saying it out loud.

"Does it matter?" Ulysses said, lifting his shoulder. "He wouldn't be the first bastard born in this town, and he won't be the last." The old man leaned forwards and patted Rafe's cheek. "And he'll have a father who loves him regardless."

Chapter Three

When Jane entered the Bennetts' kitchen mid-morning, Abby and Oliver were already discussing the best way to light a wedding dress on fire.

Did they stuff it with straw like some kind of bridal scarecrow? Should they stretch it over a basic framework like the skin mask of a serial killer? Shoot it with flaming arrows perhaps?

A cavalcade of possibilities was being tossed back and forth. And most seemed to spring from Ollie's profuse knowledge of B-grade horror movies.

"G'morning, my dear," Ulysses said, drawing her into his arms for a hug. Snuggling against the man she considered her second father, she inhaled his signature scent, the oddly comforting smell of linseed oil and turpentine. "Cuppa?"

"Coffee, please," Jane said, then took a seat at the large wooden table that dominated the centre of the room.

Jane had always loved The Forge, the Bennett family home. It was the third oldest building in Melville's Cross, after the church and the town hall, and one of only a handful of original structures still standing. Plus it had the most character.

The original house consisted of the kitchen, lounge, bathroom and what was now the master bedroom, but over the years it had been modified and expanded to accommodate the ever-increasing Bennett brood.

Now it boasted a kitchen and lounge plus three bathrooms, seven bedrooms, an art studio, a music room, a library and an internal laundry.

But the kitchen had always been Jane's favourite room, and not just because of her love of food.

The kitchen was the heart of the home, the hub, the meeting place, the place where hopes and dreams were shared over endless cups of tea and biscuits. A place of community. And comfort.

And sex.

Looking around the room as she sat beside Oliver, Jane suddenly remembered having sex on the table. And on the kitchen bench. And the floor. And once up against the pantry door.

And the man sitting opposite her, sipping coffee and stalwartly ignoring her presence, was the man she'd had sex with.

The man who'd once stripped her naked, laid her out on the table and drizzled honey over her pussy, then licked her clean so thoroughly she'd come twice from his tongue alone.

His gaze flicked up from his newspaper and locked on hers. "Jane," he said. He sounded half asleep. "How are you feeling this morning?"

Jane swallowed hard, the memory of Rafe's tongue on her body combining with the intensity of his dark blue stare and rough baritone sending a jolt of desire through her veins, waking her up in ways caffeine never could. "Fine," she breathed. "I'm fine."

Damn hormones.

She'd been left at the altar less than twenty-four hours earlier, had a fight with Rafe, barely slept a wink, and yet her body was still champing at the bit for a taste of this man.

Sucker for punishment, anyone?

Wriggling uncomfortably in her seat, she tried to find some equilibrium. And that's when she noticed Rafe's hair, or lack thereof.

Someone had attacked his preppy lawyer hairdo with a pair of clippers and a #1 blade.

He looked... good.

Real good.

Not that Rafe Bennett didn't always look good—the man was six feet and three inches of well-made male wrapped in sex appeal and dipped in *phwoar!*—but the new haircut sharpened his features, gave him an almost dangerous edge she hadn't realised was there and *damn* if her lady parts didn't stand up and pay attention.

Sucker for punishment? Lock me up and throw away the key.

Thankfully Ulysses chose that exact moment to set a mug of steaming goodness down in front of her, distracting her from her inappropriate train of thought. "Here you go."

"Thanks, Uly," she said, watching warily as Rafe's attention drifted back to his newspaper.

Looking around the table at her second family, she realised they probably all knew about the baby. More to the point, they knew who the baby's daddy was.

How could they not?

The Bennetts shared everything.

But she also knew she could trust them not to tell

anyone else until she was ready. That was one of the great things about the Bennett family—they had no time for gossips and were fiercely protective of their own.

Thankfully that included her.

"What's your preference, Janie?" Oliver asked.

"Huh?"

"How do you want to light this bitch up?" he said, pointing to the pile of cream-coloured satin and lace sitting in Abby's lap.

"Oh. Um, I hadn't given it any thought, to be honest. Just shove it in the fire, I guess. Roast some marshmallows over it." She sipped her coffee. "Ugh! This is tea!"

"Sorry, my dear," Uly said from the other side of the kitchen. "High levels of caffeine are bad for the baby."

"I only drink one a day," she groused. "And I only drink it for the flavour."

"I'll get you some decaf." That from Rafe from behind his newspaper.

Jane scowled at the broadsheet in front of her. "What part of 'I drink it for the flavour' did you not understand?"

He turned the page, still avoiding looking at her. "What part of 'caffeine is bad for the baby' did *you* not understand?"

"Arse," she muttered behind her mug of tea.

The newspaper lowered and Rafe reached for his own mug. "Mmmm... coffee."

Oooh, them's fightin' words. "You know when I told you to shave, I didn't mean your entire head."

His brow went up and his mouth tugged down at the corners. "I didn't do it for your benefit, I assure you."

Her lips thinned in a self-satisfied smile. "Thank goodness for small favours. I'd hate to think *I'm* responsible for whatever midlife crisis you're going through."

Abby hid a swift smirk behind her hand. Ollie pushed back his chair and left the kitchen, shaking his head every step of the way. Jane could have sworn she heard him mutter "Get a room" under his breath.

A minute later, she was being attacked by two unruly teenage girls. "We made you a present," they said together as they hugged her half to death.

"Can't... breathe...."

"Whoops."

"Sorry."

Diana and Josie Bennett were Charlie Bennett's twin daughters. He'd fathered them at the behest of his best friend, Amy, when she and her partner Jess hadn't been able to afford IVF treatments. Jess being bisexual and Charlie being up for pretty much anything, it hadn't taken long for the miracle of life to take hold.

Currently those miracles were thirteen years old and filled with an inexhaustible supply of youthful exuberance. Standing at six feet tall, they reminded Jane of Great Dane puppies, all long limbs and no off button. But they were also two of the sweetest, most well-adjusted girls she'd ever known.

"What did you make for me?" Jane asked as the girls sat down on either side of her.

A rough approximation of a voodoo doll was thrust into her hands. It was obviously Sam. It had brown wool stitched to its head for hair and someone— Ulysses, probably—had painted a rather striking like-ness of his face onto the calico. Several sewing pins were already sticking out of it, mostly in the groin region.

Jane smirked. "Thank you, girls. This is very... thoughtful."

"We thought you might like to burn it with your dress," Josie said.

"Or cut it into little bits, spilling its entrails onto the altar of your pain and *then* set it on fire." Everyone turned to stare at Diana. Rafe even lowered his newspaper and cocked a brow at his niece. She shrugged, unperturbed by the sudden attention. "What?"

"Don't ever change, beautiful," Uly said, chuckling as he leaned down to kiss the top of his granddaughter's head.

"So, where is everyone this morning?"

Considering the entire Bennett clan was in residence, the kitchen was shockingly empty for the time of day.

"Wolf and Sally are going over the release schedule for his next book," Abby said. "Henry's tinkering in the forge, Toby's in the garden, Amy and Jess went home last night, and Charlie is...?"

"Still sleeping," the twins said together.

"Paul and Sophie went for a run, and the last I saw of Avery and Crispin, they were in Dad's studio. No idea what they're doing in there."

"Probably making a mess," Uly grumbled.

Rafe scoffed at his father. "It's already a mess."

The old man looked offended. "I know where everything is."

"Says the man who can never find his glasses," Abby said, grinning. "Even when they're on top of your head."

Jane snickered at the good natured sniping. She'd missed this over the last few months, missed the comradery and the laughter.

The unconditional love.

"Maybe we should get you one of those chains for your glasses, Uly," Jane said, grinning at the old man. "I hear they're all the rage with people of your... ah, profession."

Uly narrowed his gaze, but it didn't dim the twinkle in his crystalline eyes. "Don't you have a wedding dress to sacrifice on the altar of your pain?"

Chairs scraped on the kitchen floor as Jane joined Abby and the twins and marched out of the kitchen. Casting a look back at Rafe, she didn't miss the grin on his face, or the swiftness with which it disappeared when she caught his eye.

Yeah. This isn't going to be weird at all.

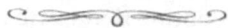

Rafe folded his newspaper and set it aside, then helped his father clean up after breakfast. They worked in near silence as they washed and dried the dishes, then wiped down the table and benches, but he knew Ulysses wouldn't stay quiet for long.

"Have you made a decision yet?"

And there it was.

"Yes," Rafe said. He'd spent all night going over his options, the pros and cons of the situation, but no matter what variables he threw into the mix, he always came to the same conclusion.

"And?" Uly pressed. "In or out?"

Rafe shook out the tea towel with a snap of his wrist, then hung it up to dry. "It's Jane," he said quietly. "Of course I'm in."

Uly smiled, his body relaxed. "Good. Now let's go watch your girlfriend set fire to her wedding dress."

Rafe released a slow, controlled breath in a bid to ease his frustration. It didn't help. "She's not my girlfriend."

"Baby mama, then. Whatever."

The roar that greeted Rafe as he exited the house was almost deafening.

His entire family had gathered in the backyard to help Jane vilify her ex-fiancé, and as he edged closer to the crowd, he discovered exactly what Avery and Crispin had been up to in their father's art studio.

A life-size caricature of Sam Lyndon, complete with wingnut ears and a boil on his nose, had been drawn on a sheet of cardboard and secured to a stack of hay bales, and Oliver was throwing knives at it.

Currently there were three blades sticking out of the makeshift Sam, one through his oversized head, one in the stomach and one in his arm.

"Your turn, Janie," Ollie said. "Just like I showed you."

Jane took her time, lined up her shot and threw the knife. It barely nicked the cardboard before tumbling to the ground, and no wonder, if Ollie had been her instructor. His brother relied too much on brute force over proper technique, and Jane had the upper body strength of a Muppet. Brute force was never going to work.

"Again," Crispin said, passing her another knife. "Aim for his fat head."

Jane threw another knife, and Rafe stifled a laugh behind his hand as the blade sailed over the top of the bales.

"I suck at this," she groaned.

"You need to focus," Rafe said, the words leaving his mouth before he could think better of it. His family split apart like the goddamned Red Sea, clearing a path for him to step forwards. *Bastards.*

"I am focussing," Jane said, more than a hint of irritation colouring her voice as he approached her.

"Give me the knife," he said sternly, knowing she'd obey him. Jane always obeyed him at times like this, when she needed—*wanted*—someone to take care of her. Whether she was willing to admit to it or not.

Jane gave him the knife, folded her arms over her chest, then stared up at him, her mouth pulled down in a sulky pout that tempted him to lean in and taste her lips, tease them apart and slip his tongue inside....

He ground his teeth together.

Do. Not. Kiss. Her.

Manoeuvring her so she—and her luscious mouth— faced Fake Sam instead of him, Rafe stood close behind her. Close enough to smell her apple-scented shampoo. Close enough to feel her tremble as he wrapped his arms around her and leaned down to speak softly in her ear.

Close enough to wish he'd kept his big mouth shut.

"You're a chef, Jane," he said, sliding his hands down her arms and showing her how to grip the blade. "Your knife is an extension of you. It does what *you* tell it to. This is no different."

"It's very different, thank you very much. I don't usually hold my knives by the blade."

"You also don't usually throw them at arseholes."

Jane snorted. "You've obviously never worked in a Michelin-starred kitchen before."

Oliver groaned impatiently. "Just throw it already."

"Quiet." Toby.

"Or we'll tie *you* to the hay bales instead." Paul.

"When did this become Pick-on-Ollie Day?" Ollie.

"When is it *not* Pick-on-Ollie Day?" Henry. Followed by snickering and the sound of a high-five. Probably Charlie.

Ignoring their audience, Rafe continued speaking soft

and low in Jane's ear. "Plant your feet, one foot forwards." He nudged her left foot with his boot. "Arm straight back, elbow bent, wrist curled." He bent her arm into position. "Now, don't let go of the blade until your hand is aligned with your arm and your arm is pointing where you want the knife to go."

Jane twisted a little in his arms and looked up at him, her gaze questioning. "How do you know so much about throwing knives?"

"Who do you think taught Ollie?" he said.

Oliver laughed. "You? Teach me? That's a hoot."

Rafe glared at his younger brother over the top of Jane's head, then leaned down again. "Also, should you somehow manage to hit Ollie," he whispered, his lips curling into a grin as they brushed the shell of her ear, "I'll eat your pussy every night for a month."

A breathy laugh had her shaking in his arms, but he felt the last of her tension ease out of her.

Stepping back and giving her space, Rafe watched Jane throw the knife again and even whooped and applauded along with everyone else when it sliced right through Fake Sam's crotch.

"Yes!" she cried out, throwing her hands in the air in victory. "Take that, you slimy prick. Quick, give me another one."

Two more knives were thrown, one stabbing into Fake Sam's thigh and the other slicing through his armpit.

"Nicely done," Rafe said with a tip of his head, adding his praise to that of his family's as they showered Jane in compliments.

"Thank you, thank you," she said to the crowd, dipping down in a curtsey. "I'm here all week." Then she marched over to Oliver and punched him in the arm.

"What was that for?" Ollie yelped, rubbing his bicep.

"For... trying to rush perfection," she said, flipping her long ginger hair over her shoulder. "Obviously."

But when she looked back at Rafe, he saw the raw need in her gaze and wondered not for the first time, *What the hell am I doing?*

Chapter Four

The Great Wedding Dress Burning turned out to be, well, pretty anticlimactic actually.

The fabric it was made from and the age of the thing meant it burned itself out in less than three minutes.

Not even enough time to toast the marshmallows Paul and Sophie had brought back from their morning run into town—which was probably a good thing considering the plume of thick black smoke and acrid stink of chemicals that had enveloped the dress within seconds of meeting the match.

Genuine silk, my arse.

The twins suggested adding the voodoo doll to the pile, which added a solid minute-thirty to the fire.

Jane had to admit watching the flames crawl across Voodoo Sam's face like some sort of living, breathing creature eating his flesh off was almost satisfying.

But she still felt unsettled. Not anxious. Not sad.

Just... off.

After the fire and some more of fun time with the

ridiculous caricature of her ex-fiancé, they all sat down for lunch. Jane tried to help, the kitchen being the one place in the world she didn't feel like a complete loser, but no one would let her.

"Put your feet up, Jane."

"We've got it covered, Jane."

"Let us take care of you, Jane."

So she sat and watched and cringed at Avery's chopping technique, then she nibbled away at her lunch, and she made small talk about nothing in particular, and she smiled.

She smiled because not smiling at the people determined to take care of her meant crying. And crying meant pitying looks, and pitying looks made her sick to her stomach.

Speaking of which.... "I'm gunna be sick."

The nearest bathroom was not near enough, so Jane raced out the front door and threw up in the garden. The taste of chicken salad and chipotle aioli soured her mouth, and she tried in vain to spit it out.

Well that was a waste of a good meal.

A minute later, a familiar voice sounded behind her. "Here, drink this."

Closing her eyes, she took a moment to gather her wits before looking up at Rafe and the glass of whatever it was he was telling her to drink. "You again," she grumbled, accepting the glass. "Are you stalking me now?"

In a move she was sure he thought intimidating, Rafe lifted his chin, raised one perfect dark brown eyebrow and stared at her. "Last I checked, you were in my house."

Feeling too ill to argue, she sniffed the glass instead. Charlie and Toby's home-brew. She took a gulp and sloshed the cold, sharp liquid around in her mouth, then gargled and spat it out. Rafe handed her a damp washcloth to wipe her mouth, and then she sat on the steps of the veranda and sipped more of the sweet, tangy ginger beer.

"Feel better?" Rafe said, taking a seat beside her.

No. "I'm fine."

He chuckled. "Liar."

Her stomach rolled again. "Fuck you, Bennett."

"Ask me nicely, Melville."

Jane did a double take. Rafe's lips were lifted in a half grin. He was teasing her again, like he had over the coffee and about hitting Ollie. As if everything was back to normal. Which it most definitely was not.

Not by a long shot.

"Please don't make me laugh," she said, forcing herself to smile, "or I just might throw up on you."

"I'll risk it." A big warm hand was suddenly rubbing circles on her back. It felt nice. Soothing. Suddenly her smile was a little less fake, her spine a little less rigid. "I was reading about morning sickness last night," Rafe said. "According to the experts, it should end soon. Unless you're one of the unfortunate few who get stuck with it for the whole nine months."

Nine months of morning sickness? *Oh, hell no.*

Jane's gaze slid sideways, her eyes wide, horrified. "Where did you read that? And why would you tell me?"

"I visited a few pregnancy and parenting websites. Maybe a forum or two," he said, shrugging his broad shoulders. "What? I like knowing things. And correct me if I'm wrong, but you did say the baby is mine. I know you don't want people knowing about that yet, but don't think for a minute I'm going to sit back and let you go through this alone. Not after I heard you throwing up yesterday afternoon. You sounded like a dying yak."

Yesterday afternoon, when he'd hidden in her bedroom

waiting to interrogate her about their impending parent-hood. *Annnd* listened to her throwing up wedding cake. "You heard that?"

"Yep."

Awesome.

Gaze narrowing, Jane continued peering up at him. She took her time and looked her fill, took in his hard planes and sharp edges. Then she remembered something else and her frown deepened.

Eventually Rafe noticed her staring. "What?"

Jane stared a second longer, then said, "Why aren't you hungover?"

His grin was instant. "Can't get hungover if you haven't had a drink."

"But in my room, you said—"

"I lied." When her mouth fell open, he shrugged. "I was angry at your assumption."

"It was a fair assumption to make. You smelled like a distillery."

He didn't quite roll his eyes. "A friend at the firm gave me a bottle of bourbon as a going away gift. It broke in my suitcase." He huffed out a sound that was half sigh, half laughter. "It was either show up at your place smelling like booze, or show up naked. I went with the lesser of two evils."

"Okay," she said slowly, remembering his behaviour as she continued giving him the side-eye and deciding he was probably telling the truth. But him being in her room at all begged a whole other question. "How did you even know I was pregnant? You weren't at the wedding and Abby promised not to tell you."

He raised that perfect brow again, silently questioning.

"I didn't want you to hear it second-hand," she said, and

if the big idiot had bothered to return even one of her bloody phone calls....

The soothing circles on her back ceased as Rafe moved to sit behind her, cradled her hips between his strong thighs. He swept her hair over her shoulder and out of his way. "Ollie texted me," he said and began massaging her shoulders and neck.

"Of course he did," Jane sighed, then closed her eyes and leaned into his magic hands. *Feels sooo good....*

"Geez, you're tense."

Glancing over her shoulder, she said, "Yeah, well, you'd be tense too if you just lost two hundred grand to a slimy fuck-hole sonofadouchebag."

Rafe's hands stopped moving. "Ahhh... how much?"

"You heard me," she grumbled, facing forwards again. "Do you know how long it took to save up that much money? Twenty-two years. And do you know how long it took that lying wankstain to empty my bank accounts? A couple of hours." Jane groaned as Rafe resumed his massage and hit a particularly tight spot.

"You've reported it to the police? Spoken to the bank?"

"That's what I was doing this morning, for all the good it'll do me. I'm never seeing that money again."

"What did Scott say?"

"Our friendly neighbourhood copper has a mate in Brisbane who might be able to help speed things along, but he wasn't hopeful. Sam is gone, his side-piece and all my money with him."

"What about the bank? Why did they let Sam move such a huge sum of money? I thought the law stated you could only move ten grand at time?"

"Unless it's a gift, or if you're buying a property, or if you're paying for something overseas, or a half dozen other reasons the bank listed this morning. And the ten grand thing is more about paying taxes than limiting how much you can move." She shook her head. "The joys of internet banking. They had all the information they needed to rob me blind and they didn't even need my signature to do it."

Rafe sighed and squeezed her shoulders. "Tell me you have insurance."

"Of course I do," Jane snapped, peeved at his lack of faith in her intelligence. "But it could be months, maybe even years before I see a payout." Her lip curled. "If I see a payout." She shook her head, her temper rising again, dragging her out of her melancholy. "I started working in the patisserie when I was ten years old, and even though Mum couldn't legally pay me, my pocket money was nothing to sneeze at. And Dad being Dad, he told me to always save ten percent of everything I earned."

"Good advice."

She shrugged. "Me being me, I saved fifty. And I got in the habit of only spending money when I absolutely had to. I mean, there's a reason I'm still driving the same car I bought when I was seventeen. I didn't know what I wanted to do back then, but I knew I wanted to do something."

"What were you going to do?" Rafe said, his warm breath brushing across the sensitive skin at her nape. She shivered and struggled to refrain from leaning against him. "Abby mentioned something about a food truck?"

Jane snorted. "Yeah, that was the plan. Street Sweets Mobile Patisserie. Has a nice ring to it, huh?"

Rafe nodded. "Yeah, it does."

"Up here in Queensland, you usually only see food trucks at big events like school fairs, the Ekka, that sort of thing. But down south, they're a part of everyday life. They even have food truck parks and websites set up telling people where to go and which trucks will be available on what days," she said, the excitement of endless possibility creeping up on her, filling her with the happiness and contentment that always accompanied a well-laid plan.

"People hire food trucks for weddings and corporate functions, all kinds of stuff. It's an amazing opportunity—" Her voice caught in her throat as reality brought her crashing back down to Earth, and her next words felt like razorblades jammed in her gullet. "It *was* an amazing opportunity. But now it's gone," she said, a sob escaping her. "Everything's turned to shit."

Suddenly needing the comfort she knew Rafe could give her, she turned and burrowed into his chest. And when his arms came around her, holding her tight, she let her tears fall unchecked.

Rafe murmured soothing words in her ear, but Jane didn't want to hear them. She didn't want to hear him say she'd be all right, or that she'd get through this, or that he was there for her.

She didn't need platitudes or sympathy.

She needed him. Rafe. His strength. His heat. His mouth. His lips. She needed action.

Needed what only Rafe could give her.

Her fingers curled in his T-shirt as she lifted her face and stared at him, her eyes darting to his mouth, to the tiny scar in the dip of his upper lip, the one no one ever noticed unless they knew it was there.

But Jane knew.

Jane knew all of Rafe's scars as well as she knew her own. And it was that one that caught and held her attention now.

Her tongue flicked out and moistened her lips.

Rafe's chest rose and fell with a steady rhythm under

her hands, and she ignored the faint rumble of warning in his voice. "Janie...."

"Rafe."

Slamming her lips to his, Jane swallowed his groan and pushed her tongue inside his mouth. He hesitated for only a moment before he was right there with her, hauling her into his lap and angling her head, using his big hands to position her exactly how he wanted her. Controlling her, claiming her with all the passion he kept so well hidden from the world. But then he stopped and broke the kiss, forcing Jane to swallow down a whimper of disappointment.

He still held her firm, his hand gripping her nape, his arm banded around her waist, but he wasn't kissing her anymore, only breathing heavily.

His forehead pressed against hers, he whispered, "It's a little too easy to fall into old habits with you."

Jane licked her lips and slid her hands over his chest. "Old habits doesn't have to mean bad habits," she said quietly, leaning closer and nibbling along his jaw, sucking on his earlobe.

"But they *are* bad habits," Rafe said with a small groan, untangling her limbs from his and shifting her to sit by his side. "And you're grieving. People do dumb things when they're grieving."

Her mouth twisted in disgust. "I am not grieving for that... that...." She struggled to come up with an appropriately awful insult. Rafe's kiss had scrambled her brain.

"Impotent, gormless fuck-knuckle?" Rafe supplied.

Jane cocked one brow at his choice of words. "Impotent?"

"I don't see him knocking you up," he said, a wry twist to his lips and an undercurrent of sarcasm in his voice.

And that's when it hit her.

Her gaze narrowed and she spoke slowly, weighing the truth of her words. "You don't believe you're the father, do you?"

He looked down at his feet. "I don't know," he said carefully.

Anger, hot and swift, rose up in Jane and she clenched her hands into fists. "You think I'm lying?"

Rafe wouldn't look at her; instead he rested his forearms on his knees and stared straight ahead at the line of trees across the road. "I think, looking at things objectively, there's every possibility your baby isn't mine."

Air burst from her mouth as though she'd been punched in the gut, and tears scalded behind her eyes. "Where was this objectivity yesterday in my bedroom when you were kissing my stomach and introducing yourself to our unborn child?"

"You've had weeks to get used to the idea of becoming a parent," he said, turning to look at her. Tight lines bracketed his mouth. "I've had less than a day. You'll have to excuse me if I need some time to wrap my head around everything."

Fuming at Rafe's turnaround in attitude, Jane's temper burst out of her in a barrage of words. "You are unbelievable, Bennett. But I tell you what, while you're sitting there wrapping your head around shit, why don't you think about this. You're the *only* man I've ever been with without a condom."

"Condoms aren't perfect," he ground out. "It says so right on the packet."

"I'm aware of that. You know what else I'm aware of?" Not waiting for an answer, she got to her feet and glared down at him. "My menstrual cycle, whom I've had sex with and when."

"I thought you were on the pill," he said, climbing to his feet and gaining the height advantage again. Jane bristled at the injustice of having to take the moral high ground from a lower vantage point.

"I was. But apparently they're not perfect either. It says so right on the packet," she said, spitting his own words back at him, then turned to go back inside.

Rafe grabbed her hand, and she hated herself for the jolt of longing that shot through her at his touch. "Where are you going? This conversation isn't over."

It was as far as she was concerned.

Yanking her hand free of his, she strode purposefully back through the front door, throwing the words over her shoulder as she did. "Pregnant lady, remember? I need to pee."

Rafe slowly released a calming breath.

At least it would have been calming if calm were a state of being even remotely achievable at that point.

As much as he appreciated—cherished, even—Jane's fiery spirit, he also loathed it at times.

Rafe hated fighting.

But growing up in a household with seven brothers and one sister who refused to be left out of anything meant he grew up doing exactly that.

Fighting for space, fighting for hot water, fighting for privacy, fighting over the last bowl of Coco Pops, and even occasionally fighting for girls.

Until that one fateful day when Jane Melville had somehow morphed from his little sister's irritating best friend into a fiery-haired goddess with creamy skin and gemstone eyes and a tight little body with a heart-shaped arse.

All other women had suddenly paled in comparison.

And how had she effected this wondrous transformation? By feeding him soup and reading him poetry.

Rafe had been sent home from university with the flu—achy joints, cold sweats, never more than two feet away from a spew-bucket flu. It was disgusting. He was disgusting.

But Jane hadn't cared.

She'd circumvented his father's quarantine order by climbing through his bedroom window with a thermos full of homemade chicken soup and a copy of Shakespeare's sonnets.

When he first saw her perfect little arse coming through the window, he thought he was seeing things, figured he was delirious with fever, but then she'd said, "Quarantine-schmarantine," and, "If you even think about throwing this up, I will never speak to you again, Bennett."

Then she'd spent the next couple of hours alternately spoon-feeding him the best chicken soup he'd ever eaten in his life and reading to him in her sensuous voice.

Shakespeare had never sounded so good, and Rafe was pretty sure he'd only kept that soup down through sheer force of will.

Now he stood in front of the toilet door, waiting for that same infuriating redhead to reappear.

"Jesus!" she gasped when she opened the door and found him staring down at her. "Are you trying to give me a heart attack? Stop following me."

Cocking one brow at her, he said, "This is still *my* house."

Her lips thinned into a scornful smile that belied the lightness in her voice. "Fine. I'll go home, then."

Rafe growled. "I don't want you to go home, Jane. I want you to talk to me."

"I don't care what you want," she said, folding her arms across the small swell of her breasts, drawing his attention to the hint of cleavage visible in the neckline of her T-shirt. "You called me a liar."

He lifted his gaze to hers and frowned. "I never said that."

"You may as well have."

"'Scuse me." Oliver shoved his way between them where they stood in the narrow hallway. "Amused spectator coming through," he said, then disappeared into the bathroom and kicked the door shut.

Rafe looked back down the hallway towards the main living area and scowled. For a household filled with over a dozen people, it was quiet.

Too quiet.

Fucking eavesdropping bastards.

Grabbing Jane's hand, he dragged her farther along the hall and then into his bedroom, locking the door behind them. "Now, where were we?"

She pulled away. "I was going home."

"Janie—"

"What?" she snapped. "You want to insult me some more?"

"That was never my intention," he said through gritted teeth, then scrubbed a hand over his scalp and stared down at her. "You never gave me a chance to explain."

Jane anchored her hands on her hips and lifted her chin. "That's because I didn't feel like listening to anything else you might have to say. In fact, I still don't."

Rafe's temper burned beneath the surface, ready to erupt. How was it he could face down hardened criminals in a court of law and not bat an eyelid, but five minutes alone with this one small woman had him ripping his hair out? What little he had left after shearing it off.

Standing almost a foot shorter than him, Jane's head barely reached his chin. She had to look a long way up to stare him down, but she could do it like no other woman he'd ever known.

And *fuck* if it didn't turn him on.

Unbidden, thoughts of her curled in his lap, her hands on his chest and her lips on his throat sprang to the forefront of his mind, and he let his gaze drop to her breasts once more.

Jane shifted her weight from one foot to the other as Rafe slowly perused her lithe figure, lingered over the swell of her stomach and itched to reach out and stroke his hands over it, to feel the life growing inside her.

A life he helped create.

Maybe.

His thoughts changed direction again, and the muscles in his throat worked as he swallowed down his desire. And his apprehension.

"I need to know, Jane," he said, his voice croaking with suppressed emotion. "I need to be certain if the baby is mine or not. You know how my brain works—I need facts, absolutes. Without them my imagination runs wild and concocts a laundry list of doubts. Please, Janie. I need to know."

A tight smile spread across her face and a devious gleam lit her eyes. "So what you're saying is, if I don't tell you what you want to know, it'll *really* annoy you?"

Rafe gritted his teeth. "You know it will. But you're missing the point."

She folded her arms again. "How much?"

Confusion pulled at his brow. "What?"

"How much will it annoy you?" she said, seemingly ignoring his statement about missing the point. "Because to be completely honest, the thought of pissing you off is pretty appealing right now."

Closing his eyes for a moment, Rafe took the time to count to ten. Slowly. She wanted to punish him for not quite calling her a liar?

Fine.

With a heavy sigh, he opened his eyes and said, "You know how much it annoys you when people call coriander 'the fancy parsley'? That's how much not knowing will annoy me."

Jane's lip curled back from her teeth and she hissed out a breath. She *really* hated the coriander thing. Just like Rafe hated not knowing for certain whom the father of her baby was.

But apparently she wasn't done torturing him yet. "Why do you want to know?" she said, making herself comfortable on his bed. Making it difficult for him to concentrate on the issue at hand as he remembered the last time she'd been in his bed. Naked, writhing in pleasure. Getting pregnant... maybe. "What difference does it make?"

"It makes a difference, Jane."

"Tell. Me. Why?" she said, not giving him an inch.

His frustration getting the better of him, he blurted out, "Because I need to protect you. Both of you. And I can't do that if I don't have all the facts. I need to know, Jane. If you have even the slightest doubt that this baby is mine, you need to tell me. Now."

"What are you talking about?" She sat up and scowled at him, at his raised voice. Probably because Rafe rarely raised his voice, and never without good reason. "What is it you think you're protecting us from?"

He blew out an irritated breath and rubbed the back of his neck. "Sam," he growled. "Or anyone else who might try to claim paternity."

Her brow scrunched. "What are you talking about?"

Rafe sighed and sat down beside her, turned to face her and spoke more gently as he tried to explain. "If I'm not the biological father, I have no parental rights to this child. I won't be able to protect them." He lowered his voice. "Not legally anyway."

He let the hint of violence hang in the air. He had zero qualms about using all kinds of non-legal means to protect Jane and her child. Not that it was prudent for a respected lawyer to advertise that fact.

Jane pulled her knees to her chest and wrapped her arms around them. "Let's say, for the sake of argument," she said, slowly, "that you're not the father. What happens if Sam, or someone else, comes calling?" She tilted her face up, the slightest wobble in her chin the only indication she wasn't as calm as she'd like him to believe. "Can they take my baby away?"

Not legally, but he kept thought that to himself. He didn't want to frighten her with the idea of someone kidnapping her child, an abhorrent act usually committed because the parent who didn't have custody wanted to hurt the parent who did.

Sometimes it involved ransom or extorting money in exchange for the safe return of the child, but generally it was nothing more than grown-arse people being petty. And it was an occurrence he saw all too often in his line of work.

"No," he said. "But unless they have a recorded pattern of abusive or antisocial behaviour, they would have the right to be in the child's life. Of course, they'd also be legally bound to pay child support."

Jane visibly relaxed, then snorted. "As if Sam would admit to anything that caused him to give money away. Anyway, it's a moot point because the baby is yours. So stop worrying."

Shaking his head, Rafe said, "The fact you felt the need to ask your hypothetical question just now tells me you're not 100 percent certain that's true. I know you said you're sure, that the timing fits, but I need to know unequivocally whether your baby is mine or not. And for the record, I don't care if it's not mine. I'm here. I'm in." He took her hands in his. "Please, Janie. Help me protect you."

Silence stretched between them as she stared at their joined hands, and if he hadn't known her so well, he probably would have panicked.

Everyone thought Jane was a tact-challenged ditz with no filter. A pretentious brat who blurted out whatever she was thinking the moment she thought it. But nothing could be further from the truth.

True, she got overexcited at times and forgot to engage her verbal filter, especially when she was stressed or upset, but who didn't? And it was true she enjoyed pushing Abby's buttons and had basically made a profession out of utilising pester-power to drag her best friend out of her comfort zone, but she'd never made Abby do anything she truly didn't want to do—karaoke, for instance, was something his sister would never agree to, even if Jane put a gun to her head.

But she also cared deeply about her friends and family and was fiercely protective of anyone she claimed as hers.

And she was smart—top three percent of her graduating class smart. Smart enough to know people would underestimate her if they thought she was a ditzy chick with verbal diarrhoea, and shrewd enough to use those misconceptions to her advantage.

Jane Melville was the devil in disguise.

Sliding her hands out from under his, she looked up at him, her face a picture of serenity. But she couldn't hide the desperation in her eyes. "What if you're right? What if—and it's a very big if—you're not the father? You said there's nothing you can do about it."

"No, I said I'd have no parental rights. I never said there was nothing we could do about it."

"So what do we do?"

"First things first, we get a paternity test done. These days it's as simple as getting a blood test. If the kid is mine, problem solved."

"And if it's not? What then?"

Rafe stood and moved out of harm's way before filling Jane in on his solution to that problem. "There is something I could do, but you're not going to like it."

She folded her arms again and raised one brow. "Oh?"

"I adopt the baby and become his or her legal guardian that way."

Her eyes narrowed. "And how, exactly, do you plan on doing that?"

Getting down on bended knee, Rafe said, "Well, first I'd have to marry you."

Chapter Five

"**A**re you out of your goddamn mind?"

Not that long ago, Jane would have jumped at the chance to marry Rafael Bennett. Hell, she would've hog-tied the big bastard and dragged him to the altar if he'd given her even an inkling of any such intentions over the past decade and a half.

But he hadn't.

So she hadn't.

And for sixteen years, they'd somehow gotten stuck on a merry-go-round of ding-dong-ditch.

But with sex.

Brain-melting, breath-stealing, turning-limbs-to-jelly, can't-walk-straight-for-days sex.

He'd visit her, she'd visit him, but neither ever stuck around beyond morning coffee and maybe a quickie. Usually not even that. And yeah, okay, maybe Rafe had a point back in May. Maybe she was the one who ran out on him more often than not, but what indications did he ever give that he wanted her to stay?

None.

Now she stared at Rafe where he knelt on the floor of his bedroom, looking up at her with his smouldering dark blue gaze and the hint of a grin tugging at his sensual lips, trying to decide if she should kiss the infuriating man or punch him in the throat.

Now he wanted to marry her? After everything that had happened?

Nooope.

Jane moved off the bed just in case her damned hormones began championing the kissing idea, because then she'd *have* to punch him on sheer principle. "I am not going to marry you," she said, wiping her suddenly sweaty palms on her jeans.

Rafe sighed. "I said you wouldn't like it."

"Then why mention it?" she snapped, anchoring her hands on her hips and shaking her head at him, still completely gobsmacked he would even make the suggestion. "Seriously? Is this your version of a joke? Because it's not funny."

Getting to his feet, he frowned at her. "It's not funny because I'm not kidding. Marry me."

"No."

"Why not?"

"Oh, I don't know," she said, throwing her hands in the air. "How about because I was jilted yesterday? Or I set fire to my wedding dress today? Too soon, Rafe. Way too soon."

"It's never too soon to put the past behind you, Jane," he said, resting his hands on her shoulders.

The only thing stopping her from rolling her eyes at him was the sincerity in his expression as he gazed down at her. Unfortunately her cynicism found another way to express itself. "*Yeaaah*, no. I'm going home now."

Thankfully Rafe didn't stop her when she unlocked the

door and escaped into the hallway, and she breathed a sigh of relief when he gently closed the door behind her and didn't follow her back out to the living room.

"Good timing," Charlie said as Jane entered the room. "We were just getting ready to leave."

"Leave?" she said, taking note of the various family members littered around the room and the piles of accompanying luggage. "Why?"

"The girls have school tomorrow," Toby said, bending down to kiss her forehead. "And I'm interviewing people all day Monday. Rebecca has decided she's not coming back to work when her maternity leave ends, so I need a new office manager."

"No more Slave Driver?" Jane said, using the nickname Toby's staff had given the woman who'd run his business with an iron fist for the last five years.

Toby chuckled. "Afraid not," he said, hugging her tightly. "Take care, sweet pea." Then he tilted his head and stared at her stomach. "May I...?" When Jane nodded, he stroked one huge hand over her baby bump and smiled. "Congratulations, Janie."

"Hey, I'll take some of that action," Charlie said. When his twin stepped away, he crouched in front of Jane, bringing his face level with her stomach. "Don't give your mother a hard time, okay, kid? Save that shit for your dad." He stood and kissed her cheek. "Oh, and we've started a betting pool, FYI," he added, then hefted three backpacks over his impossibly broad shoulders and marched towards the front door.

"About the sex of the baby?" Jane said hopefully to the rest of the room, while simultaneously praying it wasn't about guessing who the baby's daddy was. Rafe's doubts were stressing her out enough without everyone else getting in on the action. But hope died a swift death, the immediate chuckling from around the room confirming her fears.

"Nope," Ulysses said from the couch.

"We're betting on which one of you stubborn idiots gives in first," Oliver said, flopping down in an armchair. The big Viking-ish brute was immediately pounced upon by Josie and Diana, who began braiding white clover and lavender stalks into his long blond hair.

"We figure either you'll say yes or he'll stop asking," Henry continued.

Shock left Jane spluttering for a reply, partly in relief over what they were betting on, but also not. Her temper found her tongue quickly enough. "Wait, you all knew he was going to pull that marriage proposal stunt?"

Every Bennett in the room, from the teens to the septuagenarian, shrugged. "It's Rafe."

Jane could almost hear the unspoken "duh." Responsibility was the man's middle name. And apparently he felt responsible for her.

Whether the kid turned out to be his or not.

Which it is, she thought with a mental stamp of her foot.

Jane really wanted to be mad at Rafe for his bullheaded, overprotective pedanticism, for making her go through what could ultimately shatter any surviving remnants of her pride if the kid *did* turn out to be someone's other than his, but she wasn't stupid. She recognised the fact that getting a paternity test done was in everyone's best interests.

And while Rafe's dominant ways grated on every last fiercely independent nerve she owned, his taking control of the situation also calmed her mind and stopped the incessant overthinking she was prone to when she was stressed or upset, when her brain concocted a million and one ways to sweep her crap under the carpet so she could pretend it didn't exist, then built a six-foot wall around it so no one else knew it existed either.

The bottom line?

Jane didn't want to know if the kid wasn't his.

But Rafe did.

And not because he was selfish, or that he had some diabolical ulterior motive, but because he was a good and decent man.

"And for the record, I don't care if it's not mine. I'm here. I'm in."

How many men out there would say such a thing? Not many, she guessed. Even fewer would follow through on that promise. But Rafe would, and her heart melted a little at the thought he was willing to go to so much trouble to protect her and the baby.

It *was* kinda romantic.

For a lawyer.

But she'd be damned if she was going to give anyone the satisfaction of watching her soften towards him, and she certainly wasn't going to marry him just because she was pregnant.

No way was she saying yes to such a half-arsed proposal for such an archaic reason.

"What are the odds?" she said, lifting her chin and tossing her hair over her shoulder.

"Four to one Rafe caves before you do."

Mischief lit along her veins and her mouth lifted in a broad grin. She nodded at Oliver. "Put me down for twenty, my favour."

"That's our girl," Ulysses laughed. "Give him hell."

"Oh, I plan to."

Rafe came out of hiding to say goodbye to his brothers and nieces, then spent the next hour trapped in an endless parade of hugging and kissing and farewelling.

Of watching Jane smile at everyone but him while he got Scowly Jane and Peevish Jane and If-daggers-could-kill Jane.

Oh, what he wouldn't give to have Pin-up Jane back again. To watch her slide her pretty pink tongue through the frosting of a cupcake as she tempted him to replicate the motion and slip his tongue through the soft folds of her sweet pussy.

He missed that Jane.

Rafe sighed quietly, watching her chatter away with his family with an ease and familiarity that warmed his heart and urged his lips into an indulgent smile.

That was until he saw Charlie pull her into a hug and grin at him over her shoulder as his hand inched closer and closer to her pert little arse.

White-hot fury coursed through Rafe, as did the urge to pummel his older brother into the dirt for putting his hands on her.

Hands clenched into fists, he moved towards them, but before he could unleash his rage, Charlie—the utter, utter bastard—burst out laughing and released her, then lifted his hand to wave at their father. A hand he'd come dangerously close to losing.

As the last of the visitors disappeared down Bennett's Road, Rafe followed his remaining family back to the house, and Jane climbed inside her rust bucket of a Jeep.

The thought of her driving around in that thing had always given him reason to pause, but now she was pregnant, he was downright terrified.

To say her car was a deathtrap was a generous description, but the woman stubbornly refused to buy a new one. He supposed now she'd been robbed blind, she couldn't afford one anyway.

Maybe she'll agree to marry me if I buy her a new car?

Nah. That'd never work. Jane wasn't the type of woman you could bribe with a car. A shiny new set of hand-forged chef's knives though....

Rafe listened to the engine turn over with a whine, wheezing to life for a brief moment before making a clunking sound and jolting the vehicle forwards.

A car door slamming shut and the creak of the bonnet being opened quickly followed, adding to the overall orchestra of hopelessness.

"Don't do this to me, baby," Jane said, a sweet coaxing tone in her voice. "Not today."

He could imagine her speaking to her child the same way, and his gut clenched with need.

There had to be a way to convince her to accept him.

Ollie and Wolf stopped in front of Rafe, blocking the doorway into the house. They exchanged a glance, then stared at him.

Wolf shrugged. "I'd help her, but motorbikes are really more my thing. Besides, Sally threatened to shove her prosthetic leg up my arse if I don't get my final edits back to the publisher ASAP."

"And I'd help her except... I don't want to," Ollie added. "Besides, she'll never agree to marry you if you keep avoiding her." He continued down the front hallway, waving as he went. "Go get her, tiger."

"You know you have flowers in your hair, right?" Rafe called after him.

Oliver flipped him off without so much as a backwards glance.

Wolf grinned and slapped Rafe on the back, and then he disappeared down the hall too.

"Charlie and his fucking bets," Rafe muttered to himself, then turned around and headed back towards Jane and her Jeep. "Need a hand?"

Jane jumped at the sound of his voice. Her hand flew to her chest as her knees gave way, and Rafe grabbed her around the waist to keep her on her feet.

His hand brushed against the swell of her belly, and a rush of emotion washed over him.

Joy, contentment and... *pride*.

Jane shoved at his hand and took a step back. "Would you stop sneaking up on me, please? Geez."

"Sorry," he said, a sheepish grin tugging at his lips.

Her eyes narrowed. "No you're not."

His grin widened. "No. I'm not."

"What do you want now?" she said with a sigh as she turned away and leaned over the engine.

Rafe watched her push and pull and prod at engine parts he couldn't name to save his life. "Do you know what you're doing?"

"Better than you do, lawman." She stopped to look at him. "If you want to do something useful, send Ollie out to help me. At least he knows what he's doing under here."

Biting back a sharp retort about spending his formative years with his nose in a book instead of an engine, Rafe kept his voice even.

"Let me buy you a new car. Something a little more reliable."

"I don't need a new car," she said, jumping back in the driver seat and turning the key. She swore when nothing happened, then slammed the door again.

"Come on, Janie. This car is older than you."

"So are you, but you don't see me packing *you* off to the retirement home."

Rafe huffed out a sigh and threw his hands up in surrender. "Okay," he said, then got out of her way, deciding to wait for the Jeep to make the decision for her. "I'll be over here when you're ready."

He didn't know much about cars, but he knew what a dead engine sounded like. It sounded like an angry redhead damning her once faithful steed to Hell for all eternity.

With one final slam of the Jeep's door, Jane marched straight past him, making a beeline for his car.

"You're driving me home." She barked the order at him, then climbed into the passenger seat. Rafe followed her, his shoulders bouncing every step of the way as he tried—and failed—to contain his humour.

Less than ten minutes later, he was pulling into her parents' driveway. Jane hadn't said a single word the entire way, so she caught him off guard when she finally spoke.

"I don't want your charity," she said quietly, her hands clenched in her lap.

Rafe killed the engine and unfastened his seat belt. "Good. Because I'm not offering it."

"Then what do you call buying me a car?" she demanded, scowling at him.

"Providing for my family," he said, turning in his seat to look at her directly. "You need your independence, and you're going to need a safe, reliable car when the baby comes." He paused to gauge her reaction, which could best be described as cautious. "May I humbly request you donate your Jeep to science and allow me to buy you a grown-up's car?"

Bracing himself for an argument, Rafe almost laughed in relief when Jane nodded and said, "Fine. Arse. But I want it on the record that I'm only agreeing to this because it's best for the baby."

Biting back a grin, Rafe said, "Duly noted." Then he jumped out of the car and ran around to the passenger side, holding the door open and taking Jane's hand to help her out.

A small frown pulled at the corners of her mouth. "I'm pregnant, not an invalid," she muttered.

He smiled his most charming smile. "It's called being a gentleman."

"It's called being a condescending jerk."

Rafe shut the door, then crowded Jane against the side of the car, stared down at her pretty face and watched the defiance dance in her emerald eyes.

"If I didn't know any better, little girl," he said, one brow raised and a smirk firmly entrenched on his lips, "I'd say you were trying to pick a fight. Now, why would you do that, I wonder?"

A sudden intake of breath made her breasts swell and press against his chest, and that defiance he'd seen in her eyes turned molten and desirous. Wicked.

"Certainly not for the make-up sex. That would be ridiculous."

Rafe chuckled and he stroked his thumb over her plush bottom lip. Her lips parted, tempting him, inviting him to take the next step.

He pressed his body closer, felt her softness yield to his strength, but before he could even think of lowering his head and pressing his mouth to hers, her father appeared on the veranda and cleared his throat.

Jane stiffened and Rafe took a step back, but not too far. "Alec," he said, sending a perfunctory nod in the older man's direction.

"Rafael," Alec said, his arms folded tightly across his chest and his perm-a-scowl set firmly in place.

Jane stood still and silent, refusing to make eye contact with either of them, so Rafe bent down and kissed her cheek. "I'll check in with you tomorrow, okay?"

Her nod was jerky. "Fine," she said, then ran up the veranda steps and disappeared through the front door, followed closely by her father.

Rafe climbed back in the driver seat, sighed heavily and adjusted his aching cock. "Fuck."

Chapter Six

Jane sat wedged between her parents on the couch, watching a television program about wannabe bakers competing for the chance to win a golden egg whisk or something, and listening to her mother *tsk* and mutter, "Amateurs," every five minutes.

"Yes, dear," her father said absently, flicking through a magazine about wooden boat designs. "I think them being amateurs is the point of the show."

As time wore on and the next program began, Jane felt an unnerving sense of déjà vu crawl over her skin. She'd been here before, sat in this exact spot, listened to this exact conversation, wished she could be somewhere, *anywhere* else.

The last time, she'd been a teenager and too polite to move off the couch before the required allotment of "family time" had come to an end.

Now she was a thirty-two-year-old woman who was quite simply over it and had better things to do with her time.

Wanting to be alone—or at the very least, needing to be

away from the suffocating presence of her mum and dad—
Jane excused herself and retreated to her bedroom.

Being careful of her belly, she flopped down on the soft
bedding, then reached for her mobile phone... that she had
no idea how the hell she was going to continue paying for.

Awesome.

Jane unlocked her phone and scrolled through her
social media feeds for about ten minutes before morbid
curiosity got the better of her and she pulled up her banking
app.

It was only the hundredth or so time she'd checked it
since her not-wedding, but she still foolishly clung to the
hope that it had all been a bad dream, and that if she just
wished hard enough, her money would reappear and everything would be all right.

But when she saw her available balance was only
$47.28 instead of the $200,964.12 she'd had tucked away
in there two weeks ago, reality kicked her right in the feels
with the force of a Mack truck, and she thought she was
going to be sick.

Yep, nothing had changed.

Her accounts were still empty.

She was still broke.

And she still had a whole other person growing inside
her who would eventually need food and clothing and a
mother who actually had half a clue about what the hell she
was doing.

The urge to throw her phone at the wall and smash it
into a million pieces set angry tears burning behind her
eyes, mostly because she knew she couldn't afford to replace
it if she did.

Just like she'd known, as she'd listened to the dying
throes of her Jeep after lunchtime, she couldn't afford a new

car either, or rent her own place, or provide even the most basic of needs for her child.

She was going to have to rely on other people, on her parents, on Rafe, and she wasn't sure if she could. Or even if she should.

After all, there was a reason she'd never officially dated the lawman, and it wasn't from a lack of attraction.

When her father had interrupted her and Rafe in the driveway, she'd been sure he'd been about to kiss her again, despite what he'd said about falling back into old habits.

Bad habits.

She'd not imagined the look of pure hunger in his eyes when he'd trapped her against the car door and asked if she was picking a fight with him. Nor had she imagined the thick erection he'd pressed against her belly.

He'd been going to kiss her.

She knew it. And she'd wanted him to kiss her—desperately! She'd wanted to feel his firm, hot lips pressed against hers as he mastered her mouth and stole her breath. She'd wanted to inhale his cologne, that heady scent of warm leather and rich spice, and lick the strong column of his neck, feel his Adam's apple bob when he swallowed down a groan of desire....

Rafe Bennett was a confusing, contradictory man.

One moment he was pushing her away, telling her no. The next he was staring down at her, his fathomless blue eyes glazed with desire, his perfectly moulded lips quirked in a knowing grin and his big broad body looming over hers.

Making her heart race and her pussy wet.

And yes, admittedly, she *may* have been goading him into a fight. But who could blame her? She had itches that needed scratching, and she liked the way he scratched. And fights with Rafe nearly always ended in sex.

Sweaty, passionate no-holds-barred monkey sex.

But what was with the whole asking her to marry him thing? Did he honestly think she'd say yes?

Her eyebrows drew together and her forehead scrunched as she remembered how she'd felt when the words left his mouth—confused, then hopeful, then angry.

And aroused. Always aroused.

Rafe had asked her to marry him.

No, actually, not asked. Stated plainly.

Demanded, even.

"Marry me."

Not "Will you marry me?" or "I think we should get married."

Just "Marry me."

It wasn't even a question.

And she couldn't deny that a small part of her had given serious thought to saying yes. A *very* small part of her.

One that clung to the way things used to be when she was young and naïve and thought Rafael Bennett had hung the sun and the moon in the sky just for her.

Jane wasn't that girl anymore.

Taking another look at her pathetic bank balance, Jane sighed. She needed money, and she still owned enough pride to want to earn it.

She might not have enough time to save up what she'd had, but she could easily save enough to get her own place by the time the baby was due. And she had some stuff in storage she could sell online. That would get her a few extra bucks.

But what she really needed was a job.

Her mum hadn't yet hired anyone to take over her shifts at the patisserie, so she was good to go there, but one job was not going to be enough.

Opening up her email app, she sent a quick message to her boss at the catering company she'd worked for on the weekends, asking for her old job back.

After bragging about her food truck for the last couple of months, going back to work for someone else felt like admitting defeat. But what choice did she have?

She rubbed her hand over her belly.

None. She had no choice at all.

She put the phone down and rolled onto her side, stared at the shadowy corner where her reading chair sat. Where Rafe had sat after he'd climbed through her window and waited to interrogate her about the baby.

He'd looked so rough, so rugged. Wild. His hair had flopped over his eyes, and the stubble on his chin had given the straight-laced lawyer a sexy biker vibe. Very sexy. She'd actually missed it when she'd discovered him clean-shaven at breakfast. When he'd presented her with a completely new type of sexy to drool over.

Touching her lips, the memory of Rafe's kiss sprang to the forefront of her mind. She craved more. Would he have kissed her again? If her father hadn't interrupted them? Would he have risen to her bait if she'd continued pushing his buttons?

And more to the point, was he serious about eating her pussy if she hit his brother?

Desperately needing answers to her questions, Jane grabbed her phone and sent Abby a text. *Can I come over?*

Abby replied within seconds. *Depends. Who are you coming over to see?*

Her best friend knew her too well. *You. Obviously.*

Abby: *Liar *wink**

Yep, definitely too well. *Sooooo... can I come over?*

Time slowed to a crawl as she awaited Abby's response, minutes dragging on so long they felt like hours, until...

Abby: *He went to bed already...*

Jane: **sigh* of course he did.*

Abby: *... but his window is probably open.*

Jane grinned. *Have I told you lately how much I love you?*

Abby: *Not nearly enough.*

Jane: *I love you. I love you. I love you.*

Abby: *Wolf says if you're gunna bang Rafe to keep the noise down. He's on a deadline.*

Jane: *I can't promise that *wink* But I promise to try *kisses**

Rafe's eyelids cracked apart at the sound of his window being shoved open; the feminine grunting accompanying it had him rolling over to face the intruder.

Well, the intruder's arse.

Jane had obviously climbed through feet first and was leaning on the windowsill as she eased her foot onto the floor.

He reached up and flicked on the lamp beside his bed.

The plush denim-clad arse pointed in his direction froze. "Busted," she said in a sing-song voice.

"What are you doing?" Rafe said, propping himself on his elbow.

"Climbing through your window." She righted herself and turned to face him. "Duh."

"I can see that." Rafe frowned. "Why?"

She shrugged out of her coat and dropped it on the floor. Her T-shirt quickly followed, revealing a sheer black camisole that hid nothing from him, and his mouth watered at the sight of her perfect breasts and the hard little peaks atop them straining against the fabric.

"I came to collect my winnings."

His cock swelling fast, Rafe swallowed hard. "This isn't about Charlie's stupid bet, is it? Because you won't win by cheating."

"No," she said, toeing off her sneakers and unbuttoning her jeans, doing her damnedest to put him on edge. And succeeding. "This morning you said if I hit Ollie, you'd eat my pussy every day for a month."

Rafe's grin was slow but steady, spreading across his face like a languidly stretching cat. He had said that, hadn't he?

In a fit of insanity, when he wasn't really sure what the hell he was thinking or doing or saying, he'd said he would eat her pussy if she hit his brother.

He'd told himself at the time that he'd said what he did to make her laugh and help her relax, make throwing the heavy knives easier. And he'd known she wouldn't actually throw a knife at Ollie for something as basic as a tongue-tickle.

But that wasn't the whole truth.

Yes, he'd made her laugh, had felt her body soften in his arms, felt the tension leave her muscles, and she'd thrown that knife with painful accuracy. Then she'd thumped Ollie and looked at him with a hunger he knew only too well. And he'd known in that moment why he'd said what he did.

Because being there for her wasn't enough.

He wanted her. Needed her. Like he needed air to breathe. And he was willing to employ any means necessary to have her. To take her and keep her and make her his again.

Only now he was imagining using his promise of carnal delights for another purpose. As much as he wanted to lick and suck and touch, wanted to make her sigh and laugh and scream, he wouldn't. Not yet.

He wanted to fuck her. He wanted to shove his cock deep inside her willing body and take her, pleasure her, wanted to empty himself inside her and fill her tight cunt with his come.

But he was willing to wait if it helped him achieve his new goal.

When she'd walked out of his bedroom after their argument, he'd kicked himself for not handling things better. He'd wanted to protect her, and all he'd done was piss her off.

Admittedly, his marriage proposal could have been smoother. And better timed. It certainly wasn't how he'd envisioned proposing to the girl of his dreams, but desperate times called for desperate measures.

He would keep her safe.

Pushing himself into a seated position, Rafe ditched the grin and leaned against the bedhead, then yawned, feigning disinterest. "I said every *night* for a month," he said, scratching his naked chest. "And you didn't hit Ollie with a knife, so it doesn't count."

She folded her arms across her chest in an obvious move to emphasise her perky little tits, and her features set into what Rafe referred to as "full Jane mode".

A smug, knowing smile tugged at her lips, green fire burned in her narrowed gaze, and her chin lifted with an argumentative tilt. Her debating skills were impressive, so much so he'd happily set her loose in a courtroom full of barristers just so he could sit back and watch as she ate them alive. *Popcorn, anyone?*

"You never said I had to hit him with a knife."

He bit the inside of his cheek to keep from smiling again. "It was implied."

She raised one brow. "But not specified."

He'd give her that one and acquiesced with a nod. "So... you want me to eat your pussy, huh? Does that mean you accept my marriage proposal?"

She scoffed. "I think you mean do I accept your demand to marry you," she retorted, "and the answer is still no." She anchored one hand on her hip and jabbed one finger in his direction with the other. "And you never said anything about eating my pussy being conditional on any of that marriage malarkey. We struck that deal well and truly before any of that other nonsense. It's a completely separate contract."

"We never shook hands on it," Rafe said, enjoying himself way more than he should have been.

"It was a verbal contract, which I committed to when I punched Ollie in the arm."

Jane folded her arms across her chest again, that time because she was in a snit, not because she was trying to boost her assets. But she managed to distract him all the same. More so because the action was natural and not a calculated move, which was so much sexier.

"Or are you saying you're not a man of your word?"

A sudden urge to rip the rest of her clothes off and sink his tongue deep inside her sweet pussy had him slipping from the bed and prowling towards her.

Slowly he backed her up until she was pressed flush against the door, then reached around her to lock it.

Pressing his palms flat against the wooden door, he caged her between his outstretched arms. "I always keep my word, beautiful," he said, lowering his voice to the soft growl he knew turned her on. As he watched her chest swell with a sharp intake of breath, he knew it had worked. "Put your hands behind your head and leave them there."

"Don't tell me what to do." She tried to sound tough, but her voice came out breathy, sexy. Spots of pale pink coloured her cheeks, darkened her throat and ears.

Lips lifting in a predatory smirk, he murmured, "But you like it when I tell you what to do."

"I do not," she said, glaring up at him.

Her arms stayed glued to her sides, her hands clenched in fists, and he knew what game she was playing. She was trying to force a reaction out of him, get him riled enough that he'd put his hands all over her and force the issue, give her exactly what she wanted so she could be on her merry way.

But he wasn't playing that game anymore.

Rafe was playing for keeps.

"No?" he said, cocking one brow. "So you're saying if I were to slide my hand inside your panties right now, I wouldn't find you wet?"

The muscles worked in her throat. "No."

"No, you're not saying that, or no, your pussy isn't wet? Be specific, please."

Her head fell back against the door with a soft *thunk*, her eyes narrowed on his face. "No, my pussy isn't wet." Then her lips turned up at the corners and she slid her hands up his chest. "That's why I need your tongue."

Rafe chuckled, then bent his head to kiss the soft skin beside her upturned mouth. A tease. A temptation. "Such a naughty girl."

Jane whimpered, but when she turned her head to capture his lips, he pulled away and the sound became a snarl of frustration. "Kiss me," she demanded.

"Marry me," he countered.

She snarled again. "No."

"Then I guess the only lips I'll be kissing are these," he said quietly, cupping her between her legs.

She sucked in a breath and closed her eyes, and Rafe swallowed a groan as he watched her tongue dart across her bottom lip, then retreat inside her mouth.

He wanted to suck on her tongue, wanted to feel its silky slide as she wrestled him for control. A shiver ran through him at the thought, and it was taking all of his strength to hold himself back.

Jane wasn't the only one who'd have to be satisfied with less than she wanted.

All evening he'd searched for a way to persuade her to marry him, and here she was offering him a solution, one that fit quite literally in the palm of his hand.

One month. He had every night for one month to convince her to change her mind. To convince her they'd always been heading in this direction, even if she didn't know it.

Chapter Seven

Jane sucked in shallow breath after shallow breath as she tried to calm her racing heart.

Rafe had her pinned to his bedroom door, his naked, muscled torso and svelte biceps on prominent display, his thick erection straining against the soft blue cotton of his pyjama bottoms, and his big hand cupping her pussy through her jeans.

His warm breath brushed against her ear as he explained her situation in no uncertain terms. He'd lick her pussy for her, but—assuming she was reading between the lines correctly—the bastard was withholding sex unless she agreed to marry him.

He wasn't even going to kiss her.

What the actual fuck?

Needing clarification, she said, "I'm sorry... what?"

A deep rumbling chuckle shook his big body and his chest brushed against hers, rasped the filmy fabric of her camisole against her taut nipples. Her extremely sensitive nipples.

Thanks, pregnancy!

She bit her lip to stifle her whimper and sucked in another breath.

His hand was still wedged between her thighs, not moving. The heat of his skin, the constant pressure of the heel of his palm pressed against her clit made her throb with awareness.

She wanted to clamp her legs shut, to ease the pulsing ache he was causing in her heated flesh. But his hand was too damn wide, and Jane had no choice but to stay where he'd put her.

"What?" Rafe said with a shrug, not bothering to hide his humour anymore.

Her hands curled into fists by her sides. "You know what, you annoying man." She tried rocking her hips, tried forcing him to move his hand and give her what she wanted, what she needed, but he cupped her harder, squeezed her mercilessly until she yelped and ceased her movements.

"You're not going to fuck me?" she groaned, not sure if she wanted to cry or... nope. She just wanted to cry.

Tilting his head slightly to one side, Rafe quirked a brow at her, studied her face and hopefully saw the pleading in her eyes, because she'd be damned if she was going to say it out loud.

"No, I'm not." He kept his voice low as he spoke. "I'll eat your pussy every night for a month as promised, but if you want more than that, you'll have to earn it. And you want it, don't you, Jane?" He tightened his grip between her legs. "You want my big dick inside your tight cunt."

Jane squirmed against his hand, his dirty talk adding fuel to the fire, turning her on as only he knew how. *Hell yes,* she wanted him inside her. That was the whole point of her visiting his room in the middle of the goddamned night!

She wanted his big strong body holding her down, slamming into her, reminding her she was a woman, sexy and desired.

She needed to feel his lips on her skin, trailing kisses from one end of her body to the other, wanted to feel his mouth on her breasts, feel his lips pluck at her nipples, feel the heat of his tongue as he laved them with attention.

And she wanted him to look at her like he used to, when she was the centre of his universe, when she was his sun and he was her moon and he made love to her for the first time.

God, I need to get laid.

Jane hadn't told anyone—not even Abby—but she hadn't had sex in over a month. Her ex-fiancé—the filching scum sucker—had been rather skilled at avoiding spending time with her in the weeks leading up to their almost-nuptials.

She'd been too busy to think much of it at the time, had actually been glad for the reprieve, but as with everything else she'd pushed to the back of her mind, her sex drive was now racing full tilt ahead and gathering speed. Dragging with it a desperation she was finding hard to hide.

To say she was horny was to grossly underestimate the situation.

And Rafe wasn't helping.

"Yes." The word hissed out of her. "Yes, I want you to fuck me. Please."

"How do you want it?" he growled in her ear.

"Hard," she whispered back. "I don't care how as long as you do me hard."

A sinister chuckle filled the air around her. "Ask me nicely."

She froze. "I beg your pardon?"

"Ask me nicely to fuck you, Jane."

He wanted her to beg for his body? He hadn't done that

in a long time. Clenching her jaw to stop herself from snapping at the exasperating man, she spoke through gritted teeth. "Please, Rafe, will you fuck me?"

He smiled, but it wasn't the smile she wanted to see, the lopsided grin that came with a cheeky glint in his eyes and promised she was about to explode with pleasure.

No, this smile made her hold her breath with apprehension.

"No," he said, shaking his head.

Jane lifted her chin and hoped he didn't see it wobble. She was riding the edge of her emotions and felt like she might topple over the side at any moment. "No?"

"No."

Angry tears pricked behind her eyes. "Then what was the point of all this?" She spat the words at him and shoved at his chest. He didn't move.

The sinister smile returned as he repeated his earlier command. "Put your hands behind your head and leave them there."

What? "Are you kidding me?"

"If you'd simply done it the first time I told you, you'd be well on your way to an orgasm by now."

Releasing a slow, steadying breath, she said, "You're an arsehole."

But as she moved to obey him, tucking her hands behind her head and threading her fingers together, his smile softened and his pupils dilated, as though the action pleased him. As though she'd made him... *happy*. And warmth flooded her chest.

"Yes," he said. "But I'm an arsehole who's going to make you come all over his face."

When she finally obeyed his order, Rafe wanted to plaster his lips to Jane's and drown in the taste of her. But he didn't. He couldn't. If he wanted his plan to work, he had to stay in control of himself, hold himself back just a little.

He had to make her want him, make her crazy for him.

All of him, not just his dick.

Keeping his eyes locked with hers, he reached down and unzipped her jeans, then slowly dragged them down, helping her step out of them when he reached the floor.

Casting the denim aside, he knelt at her feet, grinned up at her as he tucked his fingers under the waistband of her black lace panties and pulled them down too.

But his grin faded fast.

Jane stared down at him as he stripped her lower half, the look in her eyes the same as it had been after she'd thumped his brother.

Hunger.

Want.

Need.

He could practically feel the desperation sluicing off her, and the urge to pick her up and cradle her against his chest, to comfort her, almost made him abandon his plans.

Then he noticed her arms and how hard she was trying to keep her hands behind her head, how determined she was to follow his orders, and his cock grew impossibly hard.

Rafe enjoyed being in control, especially in bed, but he wasn't as dominant as his brothers or future brother-in-law. And while Jane was an adventurous lover who enjoyed rough sex, her submission was more playful than painful.

So for her to surrender control to him this way, even with something as simple as keeping her hands behind her head, Rafe wanted to reward her.

"Open up for me, Janie," he said, keeping his voice low.

"Rest your thigh on my shoulder." Teeth gnawing on her bottom lip, she looked nervous, doubtful. He knew why. Jane was small and lithe, but she wasn't the most graceful of women. And she was terrified of heights. Stroking his hands up and down her thighs, he added, "If you fall, I'll catch you. I promise."

Finally she nodded and lifted her leg into his waiting hands. Rafe manoeuvred her thigh onto his shoulder, then looped his arms around the backs of her legs, both keeping her steady and holding her open to his mouth.

As always, Jane's mound was waxed smooth except for one perfect triangle of tight ginger curls. He grinned and nuzzled into it, inhaled her musky scent deep into his lungs. Chuckled as Jane's hips thrust forwards and nudged his chin.

"Patience, beautiful."

She made a strangled sound and whispered, "Please."

He chuckled, then whispered back, "As you wish." And thrust his tongue deep between the folds of her pussy.

Jane's gasp was music to his ears and it spurred him into action. Every lick with the broad side of his tongue, every flick across her clit earned him another reaction, a moan, a sigh, a panted breath. And every time he suckled her flesh, every time he took her clit into his mouth—suck, release, suck, release—she gifted him with a lusty cry of passion. Her body was his to master, his to play with and pleasure.

"Rafe." His name was a groan on her lips.

He pulled away only long enough to answer. "Yes?"

Her body jolted as he plunged back in and doubled his efforts. Suck, release, flick, suck, release, grind....

Her back arched and she cried out, "Oh, God!" But her hands stayed tucked behind her head.

Good girl.

Over and over, Rafe repeated the pattern, purposefully avoiding touching her more than necessary to get her off. Usually he would finger her as he laved her with his tongue. First one digit, then two. Sometimes three depending on how much she begged him for it.

But not this time. He'd make her come with nothing more than his tongue and his teeth and the rough stubble shadowing his chin.

Suck, release, flick. Suck, release, grind....

Her breathing was growing manic, her breaths getting shorter, more frantic. She was close. Ready to explode.

He flicked his tongue faster, sucked her clit harder.

"Please," she chanted. "Please, please, please. Oh, God. Oh, Rafe. Please!"

He gave one last hard suck on her clit, and Jane shattered all around him. She screamed as she came and her legs shook, and Rafe tasted her honeyed warmth as it slipped over his tongue and down his throat.

She tastes amazing.

True to his word, he didn't let her fall. He held her steady until her body stopped shaking, then lifted her leg off his shoulder. He made sure both of her feet were firmly on the floor before letting her go and rising to stand before her.

"Good girl," he murmured, smiling down at her, resisting the urge to stroke her cheek. "You can put your hands down now."

Rafe bit back a groan when she complied, his cock jerking in his pyjama pants, reminding him it was still painfully erect and in desperate need of relief. But he forced himself to ignore his discomfort.

Giving up his own orgasm was worth it just to see the blissed-out look on Jane's face as her arms fell to her sides and her legs trembled, threatening to give out on her.

He stood close enough to catch her should she collapse but still refused to touch her, no matter how much he craved the feel of her perfect little body tucked in his arms.

He fetched her panties and handed them to her.

Her chin wobbled and she looked away as she snatched them from his outstretched hand. "You want me to leave?"

Her voice shook, and Rafe could hear the despair in her words, see the utter wretchedness on her face.

He'd assumed she'd want to leave—she always wanted to leave—but he was never more happy to be wrong. Usually he had to coax her into spending the night with the promise of coffee and more sex.

"Do you want to stay?"

She sniffed. "Not if you don't want me to."

Rafe smiled. "I want you to," he said quietly. "But no sex, okay? Or coffee," he added, remembering their argument over breakfast.

Jane nodded and slipped her panties on, then grabbed her smartphone from her coat pocket and climbed into bed. "You coming?" she said, obviously noticing he hadn't moved a muscle in any direction.

He couldn't move.

The sight of Jane in his bed again, her long ginger-blonde hair trailing over her shoulders and spread across his pillows, her small breasts—and now her baby bump—pushing at the sheets, creating little hills and valleys for him to explore.

Or not, as the case may be.

Climbing in beside her, he decided not touching her was not going to happen. Mostly because there was zero chance he could keeps his hands off her in such close proximity and not go completely mad.

So he'd eat her pussy, and yeah okay, touching and

kissing were permissible, but the no-sex rule stayed. He wanted her to want him the way he wanted her.

He wanted her to remember all the non-bedroom-related reasons they were so good together, and if that meant cock-blocking himself, so be it.

Jane turned to face him. "I'm supposed to be helping Mum at the shop tomorrow morning."

Rafe adjusted the blankets to cover the both of them more evenly. "What time?"

"Five o'clock." When his only response was a raised brow, she shrugged and said, "Bakers."

He snorted. "Okay." He usually got up at five-thirty for his morning run anyway. Getting up a little earlier wouldn't kill him. He turned off the lamp. "I'll drive you to work."

"Okay," she said, then rolled onto her side, facing away from him.

Rafe snuggled against her and wrapped his arm around her waist, felt that innate sense of pride wash over him again as his hand settled on her stomach. He pressed a kiss to her shoulder.

"Rafe?"

"Yeah?"

A soft sigh escaped her. "Why don't you want to fuck me?"

Rafe chuckled and Jane stiffened in his arms. "I do want to," he said, nuzzling into the fall of her hair, breathing in the scent of apples. "You know I do. But I told you back in May, I can't be your rebound fuck anymore."

"That's not what this is," she said quietly.

"No? As you so rightly pointed out this afternoon, you were jilted yesterday. If crawling through my window in the middle of the night demanding oral sex isn't you on the rebound, then I don't know what is." He pumped his hips forwards and thrust his still-hard cock against the crease of her arse. "Of course, if you really want sex that bad...."

"I'm not going to marry you just so you'll have sex with me," she said, and he could practically hear her rolling her eyes at him. "Your dick isn't that spectacular."

"Firstly, my dick *is* that spectacular. And secondly, I don't want you to marry me just for the sex."

"Well I don't want you to marry me just because I'm pregnant."

Ah. So that's what this is all about. "Oh, Janie," Rafe sighed, pressing another kiss to her shoulder. "You're so much smarter that."

Chapter Eight

Jane's alarm went off at four, a shrill beeping sound she was guaranteed not to sleep through.

Nor would anyone else sleeping nearby, as she discovered when a very grumpy Rafe blindly swung his arm around looking for the button that would shut it down.

"*Faaark*," he growled. "Where is the bloody thing? Janie?"

"It's here," she said, snickering. "I've got it."

Jane slid her finger over the screen of her smartphone, silencing the alarm, then checked her weather app and read her emails. And wanted to scream.

"Shit!"

Within seconds, the bedside lamp was on and Rafe was sitting bolt upright, suddenly very awake and staring down at her with concern.

"What is it? What's wrong? Are you going to be sick?"

His hand went immediately to her belly, settling so gently over her baby bump she almost forgot to breathe.

So protective.

She'd also forgotten how unbelievably sexy he looked when he'd just woken up. With those bedroom eyes and a bit of scruff on his chin, his strong, naked torso on full display and his new bad-boy hair cut begging her to run her fingers through the short soft strands....

She forgot what she was going to say.

Her mouth flapped open and shut a few times before her brain kicked back into gear and she remembered how to form sentences again.

"No, not sick. I got an email from my boss at the catering company in Brisbane," she said, dragging her eyes away from his muscled chest and focussing on his stern face. "She's already hired someone to replace me on the weekend roster."

"Oh," Rafe said, as if it wasn't a big deal, and flopped back on his pillow. "Is that all?"

Dropping her gaze back to the phone in her hand, she sighed heavily. "Damn it," Jane muttered quietly as she read through the particulars of the email again. *Sorry to disappoint you... if you'd only contacted me earlier... will let you know if something comes up... blah, blah, blah.*

Fabulous. "This is a problem for me, Rafe."

"What's the big deal?" He yawned and stretched his long body, his huge feet catching in the sheet and dragging it down, revealing his morning hard-on to her desiring gaze. "You still have the job at the patisserie."

"The big deal is that I'll never be able to save enough money in time with only one job," she said, her mouth watering at the sight of his tented pyjama pants.

So. Fucking. Horny.

Stupid hormones.

His gaze narrowed under a furrowed brow. "Enough money for what?"

"To move out of my parents' house before the baby comes."

"And why is that so important? Wouldn't it be better to stay somewhere with people who care for you, people who can help out with the baby?"

If she didn't know Rafe so well, she might have missed the hint of calculation in his voice, but she'd been around him her entire life and knew there was very little the man left to chance. He was probably already figuring out how to solve her problems for her.

Because obviously she sucked at adulting and needed a big strong man to help her out.

Wow. Where did that snarky thought come from?

Stupid emotions.

Jane couldn't deny the fact she felt like a total loser. A week earlier she'd had goals and plans and a mission statement.

She'd scrimped and saved and worked two jobs to make her dream a reality, and now here she sat, ripped off, knocked up, let down and screwed over.

And she hated it, hated feeling so helpless, so hopeless. But there was some fight left in her yet.

Squaring her shoulders, she made a decision. She might not be able to change the past, but she didn't have to let it dictate her future either.

It was time she pulled on her positive pants!

And her first order of business would be moving out of home. Again. But to do that, she needed money, and to get money, she needed a job. Preferably two.

"I haven't lived at home since I graduated from high school. And the only reason I've been staying there is because we gave up the lease on the cottage over by the golf course because we were supposed to be moving to

Melbourne. Do you have any idea how embarrassing it is to be living with your parents at the age of thirty-two?"

Rafe stared at her and blinked, a bemused expression blanketing his face, and she realised what she'd just said. Abby, Oliver and Rafe, at the ages of thirty-two, thirty-five and thirty-seven respectively, all still lived in their father's house.

"Not that it's a problem for some people," she said, desperately trying to backtrack. "For you guys it's more of a tradition than it is a chore, and Ulysses is awesome. Who wouldn't want to live at home if their dad was a famous artist? And—"

"Jane."

"Shutting up," she said, her cheeks heating with embarrassment.

Sitting up again, Rafe shook his head, a lopsided grin lifting his lips. "You don't ever need to censor yourself around me. You know that. I'd simply forgotten how cute you are when you ramble on like a crazy person," he said, then slid his hand around her nape and pulled her closer, narrowing her field of vision and forcing her to focus. His hand was warm, his voice deep, hypnotic.

"I meant you could move in here. It's not like we don't have the room—even with so many of us mooching off our father," he added, his amusement shining in his eyes. "And you'll be surrounded by people who care for you and can help out with the baby. Not to mention all the other benefits," he said, his gaze dropping to her mouth, his hand tightening on her nape.

Eyes narrowing, Jane tightened her lips into a thin line. "And what other benefits would those be?"

He pulled her closer, making it plain he intended to kiss her.

Placing her small hand in the centre of his solid chest, she pushed him back, knowing full well he let her do it. She'd never have the strength to push him away if he didn't allow her to.

"I thought you said if I wanted more than your tongue in my pussy, I had to earn it."

"I changed my mind," he said, trying again to cement his lips to hers.

Her heart rate increased, her eyes widened and her pussy clenched in anticipation. "We can have sex?" she blurted.

"No," he said sternly, and her bubble of hope deflated faster than a burst soufflé. "No sex. I just thought we could fool around like we used to. *Before* we started having sex. You remember what we used to get up to, don't you, beautiful?"

Oh he just thought, did he?

And of course she remembered. Rafael Bennett may not have been her first kiss, but he sure as hell spent a lot of time helping her perfect her technique. She'd never known a man who loved kissing half as much as Rafe did.

Maybe it's time I put that knowledge to good use.

Tightening his grip on her neck again, Rafe pulled her close, tilted his head, but before their lips could touch, Jane slid her hand between them and pressed her fingers against Rafe's mouth. "I don't think so."

"I beg your pardon?" he said, the surprised tone in his voice matching the look on his handsome face.

Displaying her haughtiest of expressions, Jane continued, "I'll allow you to eat my pussy every night—"

"Oh, you'll *allow* me, huh?" His surprise gave way to a wickedly decadent smile.

"It's the least I can do," she said with complete sincerity.

Rafe bowed his head. "You're very generous."

"Thank you," she said, tipping her head in kind. "But if you want more than that—kissing, for example—you'll have to earn it. And you want to kiss me, don't you, Rafael?"

Muscles ticked along his jaw, in his cheeks, and his smile slipped as she threw his own words back at him. "And how exactly do I earn your kisses?"

"Easy. You just have to stop asking me to marry you."

Lips twisted in irritation, Rafe said, "Yeah, that's not going to happen."

"Then I guess the only lips you'll be kissing are these," Jane said, letting her legs fall open. The flare of his nostrils and instant look of hunger in his eyes was extremely gratifying.

Rafe's smile was slow to return, but seductive, almost smug. "I said I'd only eat your pussy at night-time."

Turning to look out the window, she shrugged and said, "It's still dark outside. It counts."

"You know this means war, right?" He chuckled as he slid her panties off and positioned himself between her legs.

She snorted. "I reckon I can hold out longer than you can."

His answer was a slow lick along the length of her sex with the flat of his tongue, followed by a hard suck on her clit. A shock of sensation lit through her and she sucked in a lungful of air. The second pass of his tongue made her leg twitch and her resolve stumble.

Rafe chuckled again. "We'll see."

Rafe dropped Jane at the patisserie just as her mother, Mary, was flicking on the lights. Straight To The Hips Café and Patisserie was founded by Mary's grandmother in 1950 and was one of the few buildings in town that didn't have the name "Melville" stamped on it somewhere.

It was a fantastic old building made from rough-cut sandstone blocks with big storybook windows and a glass-pane door.

Every birthday, graduation or special occasion—which in the Bennett household could simply mean it was a Tuesday—Ulysses would bring Rafe and his brothers and sister here for milkshakes and cake.

And it was here in this shop that Rafe first noticed Jane —or more to the point, she'd made her presence known to him.

He'd known her since she was born, of course—in a town of less than one thousand people, everyone knew everyone—but it was around the age of three that Jane apparently decided an eight-year-old Rafe looked like he'd be fun to climb and steal cake from.

He'd always figured it was because he was the shortest of the younger Bennett boys and looked less intimidating than Charlie, Toby and Oliver. Or it could have been the fact he wasn't as rowdy as Charlie and Oliver, and wasn't as terrifyingly silent as Toby.

Either way, Rafe seemed to fall inside her Goldilocks Zone, and she took every opportunity to make sure he knew it.

Later in life, she'd become a right pain in his arse, teasing him about girls, about his height, about his own annoying habit of correcting people all the time, because unerring accuracy was apparently something to be ashamed of.

But then one day chicken soup and Shakespeare happened and changed his life forever.

"Are you coming inside?"

He smiled at the huskiness of her voice. He'd made her come hard and fast—*twice*—before letting her out of bed, using his teeth, tongue, lips and fingers to wring her pleasure from her.

Yeah, he'd won that battle.

But not the war.

He slid his arms around her and pulled her close, the light spilling from inside the shop not enough to illuminate their faces, and the shroud of night still dark enough they needn't fear being seen.

"I really want to kiss you," he murmured against her soft hair.

"I really want to fuck you," she whispered back. "Too bad you keep asking me to marry you."

Rafe grinned. "You do realise the quickest way to make me stop asking you to marry me, and therefore get laid, is to actually, you know, marry me?"

She scowled at him. "You're evil."

His grin widened. "Your point?"

"I have work to do," she said, patting his cheek and pulling out of his embrace. He missed her warmth immediately.

He didn't let her go too far. "Hey," he said, quietly. "I was going to make appointments for us with the doctor for those blood tests. I thought maybe we could go together, unless.... Do you still want to keep it a secret?" He couldn't quite meet her gaze. "Do you still want to keep *me* a secret?"

Jane pressed the palm of her hand against his cheek and Rafe unashamedly leaned into it, absorbed her warmth and breathed in the clean scent of her skin.

She lifted one shoulder in a small shrug, smiled as she conceded. "No one can keep a secret in this town anyway."

His answering smile was slow as relief washed over him, and his chest sagged as he let go of the breath he'd been holding. "Thank you, baby."

Jane ducked her head at his use of the endearment but he didn't miss the smile playing around the corners of her pretty mouth.

Rafe knew some guys got off on the whole secret lover gig, but he wasn't one of them. Not that he wanted everybody to know his business either, but in a town as small as Melville's Cross, gossip was inevitable, and as a Bennett—the most gossiped about family in town—he had more reason than most to hate it.

The fact Jane was willing to open herself up to that type of criticism for him spoke volumes.

"I'll pick you up after work?" he said, unsure what her answer would be and hating himself for his uncertainty.

These were uncharted waters he was testing, and as much as he wanted everything to be smooth sailing, this was Jane Melville he was dealing with, and she never did the expected.

"Sure," she said, a coy smile lifting her lips. "I finish at one o'clock. Come inside when you get here and I'll make you something to eat, okay?"

Smiling, he buzzed a quick kiss over her forehead. "I'll see you then, beautiful." Then he got in his car and drove home.

Two hours later, he'd been for his daily run, showered, eaten breakfast, fought off an interrogation from his sister about the strange noises she'd heard coming from his bedroom the previous night—*like she can talk*—and was now unlocking the door to his new office.

His new, overcrowded, unorganised office.

When Mayor Rose had asked Rafe to consider moving

home and taking over the job of town counsel, she'd warned him the previous bloke had been a bit of a pack rat, but this?

If there were a level of Hell dedicated to filing, Rafe was pretty sure he'd found it. He didn't he even know where to begin to sort this shit out.

As he waded through the maze of paper, he kicked himself for not coming down sooner and taking a look, but he'd been putting it off, wanting to enjoy a few precious days relaxing and spending some quality time with his family. Reconnect with everyone on the rare occasion they were all in the one place.

He should have taken a look back in May when the mayor approached him in the first place. But the only thing on his mind that day had been a hot little redhead, her cupcake-licking skills and counting down the minutes until he could get her alone and naked.

And then they'd fought, and he'd gotten drunk and Charlie and Toby had dragged his sorry arse back to Brisbane to sleep off his hangover and regret.

It wasn't until he discovered Jane planned to move to Melbourne that he'd accepted the mayor's invitation, and then he'd done literally anything to avoid going back to Melville's Cross until he absolutely had to.

Which just so happened to coincide with Jane's wedding day.

Because he was a masochist.

He'd watched from afar as she'd arrived at the church in a cherry-red Mustang convertible, looking so happy his heart hurt. He'd wanted her to look that happy with him.

To *be* that happy with him.

Someone must have heard his prayers that day because the next thing he knew, his phone was vibrating a hole through his pocket, receiving a barrage of text messages from Oliver about Sam doing a runner and oh, by the way, Jane's pregnant.

He still wasn't sure which of his emotions had been the more overwhelming when he'd read those words: his anger at Sam Lyndon for proving him right, his elation at the thought he might be a father, or his frustration at not being able to go to Jane, to rescue her from her predicament. And then he'd broken into her house and made things worse.

But fate had handed him a second chance, and this time he wasn't going to screw it up.

Yes, it was undoubtedly "too soon", as Jane had said, for her to be with someone else. And yeah, when the gossips found out about the baby, there would be fallout to contend with, but they were stronger together than they were apart.

If he could only convince her to make that togetherness more permanent this time.

After ploughing his way through the downstairs offices and the upstairs storage areas, Rafe managed to find a desk to sit at and scribbled down a to-do list. And his first item of business was to enlist some help.

A couple of phone calls followed by a few hours of trudging boxes of God-only-knew-what from one room to another, and by the time one o'clock rolled around, he was more than ready to call it quits.

His office was on the opposite side of the village green from the patisserie, and a quick jog put him in the shop at five after one.

"You're late," Jane said, flicking her gaze to his as she continued doing whatever she was doing behind the counter.

As always, Rafe's pulse ticked a little faster at the sight of her. He grinned. "Sorry, beautiful."

Conversations quietened throughout the café, and from

the corner of his eye he saw those sitting closest to him straighten in their chairs, no doubt eager to hear more.

Let the Melville's Cross Gossip Challenge begin.

Jane shook her head and sighed, but that secretive smile still played on her lips. "Take a seat," she said, using a large chef's knife to point at an empty table in the back. "I'll be there in a tick."

He settled in and watched his woman work. And his cock grew painfully hard. There was just something about a woman who knew her way around a knife that he found incredibly sexy, and he desperately wanted to kiss her. *Hard.*

But kissing her meant not asking her to marry him anymore, and he wasn't ready to quit pursuing her on that front quite yet.

A minute later she slid a plate on the table in front of him. "Eat," she said, sliding into the chair opposite his.

"Is that what I think it is?" He stared at the elegantly served dessert, drool pooling in his mouth.

"If you think it's a toasted coconut crumb base filled with a sweet yet tart curd made from lemons, limes and blood oranges, topped with fresh merengue and baked until golden, served with passionfruit and mango coulis and candied mango slices, then yes, it's exactly what you think it is."

His favourite.

Lips lifting in a slow smile, he said, "You made Rafe Pie?"

It was actually named tropical sunset pie, a concoction she'd created one night in his apartment kitchen after a couple glasses of wine and a few hours of great sex. He had memories of her prancing around his kitchen wearing nothing but an apron and a smile, and even more memories of bending her over the kitchen bench and fucking her senseless.

Racing the oven timer as they chased their bliss.

That was a really good night.

Definitely worth repeating.

"Don't let it go to your head," she said, pulling him from his memories.

"Aren't you eating?" he asked, slicing his fork through the buttery texture of the dessert. She hadn't eaten breakfast either, claiming she still felt nauseous, but he saw the excuse for what it was: nerves.

She was nervous about going back to work so soon after giving the town so much to talk about, knew once they saw her expanding belly they'd have even more fat to chew. She also knew they'd sit in her shop and look down their noses at her while she was forced to be polite to them, make small talk and not spit in their food.

Jane shook her head as she climbed to her feet again. "I'm not hungry. But you eat up, okay? And give me ten minutes," she said. "Renee's running late for her shift."

"And you gave *me* crap about running late."

"I have to keep you on your toes," she said, winking.

And as she disappeared behind the counter again, Rafe heard something he really wished he hadn't.

"Slut."

That was one part of small town living he hadn't missed.

Rafe put his fork down and pushed to his feet.

Chapter Nine

"I beg your pardon?"

Jane heard the thunderous anger in Rafe's deep voice as clearly as she'd heard the whispered slur the women at table four had thrown out as she'd passed them on her way to the kitchen.

"Shit," her mother muttered, staring out from the kitchen door. "I was afraid this would happen."

Cocking one brow, Jane said, "You were afraid Rafe would get pissy with Patricia Leighton for calling me a slut?"

Mary's lips pressed together in a flat line. "No, baby, I was afraid you coming back to work so soon would have the bitch brigade out in force, talons sharpened and tongues wagging. And that woman is the worst of them."

As far as Jane was concerned, Mrs Leighton was the human equivalent of a poodle, all long limbs and coifed hair, smarter than her prissy appearance led people to believe and downright nasty when the mood struck, which seemed to be 100 percent of the time she was in the presence of a Melville.

And was exactly why Jane was determined not to let the spiteful comment get to her.

At least she could try.

Bitch.

"I hate to say it," her mother continued, "but between the fiasco at your engagement party and you getting jilted, you've given the people in this town more to talk about in the last six months than anyone else has in years."

"You can blame Richard for the incident at my engagement party," Jane said, slipping her apron off and hanging it on a hook on the kitchen wall.

"Oh, I do," Mary assured her.

"And as for them calling me a slut, well, it's not like they have fulfilling sex lives of their own to talk about, is it?"

"Unlike their husbands," Mary muttered, frowning at the women sitting around table four. "And which one of them called you a slut? I'll spit in her food."

Jane snorted at the hollow threat. "You'll do no such thing."

Her mother made an annoyed sound. "No, probably not. Maybe I'll just use full fat milk in their coffee instead of skim, ruin their diets one cuppa at a time. It's not like any of them can tell the difference anyway," she said. "They shove chocolate eclairs and raspberry friands down their gullets like they're going out of fashion."

Chuckling at her mother's version of guerrilla warfare, Jane kissed her cheek. "Thanks, Mum. I appreciate it."

"Anytime, baby," she said. "But listen, I want you to do two things for me, okay?"

"Sure. What do you need?"

"First and foremost, get your boyfriend out of here before he causes an incident. The last thing I need is the active-wear mafia deciding to go elsewhere after their power walks just because Rafael said something to offend one of them, no matter how much they deserve it."

Jane smirked. "Yeah, I'm pretty sure that ship has sailed."

Rafe had caused an incident the moment he'd called her "beautiful" and publicly laid claim to her. And she found she couldn't bring herself to be angry at him for it. She had agreed to let the truth be known about her baby, after all, but she hadn't anticipated Rafe grabbing that acknowledgement with both hands and running through town with it for all to see.

He was usually much more private than that.

The fact he was stepping outside his comfort zone for her made her heart melt. Just a little. And that was when she realised her mother had called him her boyfriend and her first instinct hadn't been to deny it.

Well, okay then....

"Besides," she added, giving herself a little shake and getting her brain back on topic, "Straight To The Hips is the only patisserie in town. The only other place they can get a coffee and cake even remotely as good as ours is from Dieter at The Black Forest Café, and they know it. And Dieter only opens for lunch and dinner. Rafe could offend them 'til the cows come home and what are they going to do about it? Lower their so-called standards and visit the bakery for a sausage roll and a can of Coke? I don't think so."

Mary sighed. "You might be right."

"I know I'm right. What's the second thing?"

"Take the rest of the week off. You need time to process everything that's happening to you, emotionally and physically. And you and Rafe need time to figure out what's going on there too. Or did you think I didn't see you two cuddling this morning out there on the footpath?"

Renee chose that exact moment to bustle through the kitchen door. "Who was cuddling on the footpath? What did I miss?"

Realising where Mary's "boyfriend" comment came from—and more than a little curious why her mother wasn't more upset by the development—Jane blushed and ducked her head, avoided Renee's questioning stare and her mum's knowing gaze.

"I should go," she said, before Mary could make any other potentially embarrassing observations. She didn't move quickly enough.

"You've always been drawn to him," Mary said quietly, more to herself than Jane. "Even when you were little." Then she lifted her head and smiled. "And him to you."

I guess that answers that question.

Mary tilted her chin at the door. "Go on. Get out of here."

With another kiss on her mum's cheek, Jane returned to the shop floor and found Rafe waiting for her, leaning against the service counter with his arms folded over his chest and his ankles crossed, glaring at table four.

If looks could kill.

"I'm ready to go home now," she said, trying to keep her voice light enough so as to not let the women know they'd gotten under her skin, yet firm enough to jolt Rafe out of his silent crusade to defend her honour.

He relented when she laid her hand on his arm, and they turned to leave. But just as they made it to the door, she caught another snippet of amused, hateful twittering.

"... next generation of Bennett whores."

And before she could stop him, Rafe turned on his heel and confronted the spandex-clad harpies, fury dancing in his eyes. "Don't you *ever* speak about Jane that way again."

Patricia Leighton smiled, smug. Like a toad. "And what are going to do about it if I do, hmm?" she said, raking a disdainful look over Jane from top to bottom as she did, making her feel crumpled and worn.

Rafe's answering smile would have made the Devil himself shit his pants, and as the silly woman finally realised her error, she visibly recoiled from him.

His voice was soft when he spoke, and deadly calm. "Until quite recently, Mrs Leighton, I worked for the law firm that handled your latest divorce. Remind me. What's that old saying about people who live in glass houses?"

Her face drained of colour and she dropped her gaze. "Come on, Steph, Liz," she said to her cohorts as she grabbed her handbag and got to her feet. "Their food tastes like shit anyway."

"You are what you eat," Jane said as they walked past her, flashing the brightest, fakest smile she owned.

The woman named Steph stopped and glared at her. "What did you say?"

"Bon appétit," Jane replied, her smile not faltering for even a moment.

The women shoved their way through the door, throwing complaints over their shoulders as they did.

"You are what you eat, huh?" Rafe grinned, then leaned down to whisper in her ear. "Are you calling me a pussy?"

Jane burst out laughing, her smile finally real, and the tension she didn't realise she'd been hanging on to eased from her body.

"You're an arsehole."

His grin didn't falter. "Hmm, kinky."

Shaking her head at him, a little baffled and a lot turned on by his uncharacteristically public playfulness, she said, "Let's go. You're driving me home."

113

Rafe followed Jane inside her parents' house and shut the door behind them. The house was quiet, and he scanned each room they passed with a watchful eye.

"Where's Alec?"

Jane's father was a semi-retired GP and split his time between working at the doctor's surgery and restoring wooden boats for the wealthy elite living along the Sunshine Coast. Mostly for people who had zero idea about how to actually sail the damned things.

He had a long-standing rivalry with Rafe's own father, though Rafe had no idea why, and Alec hated Rafe for something he didn't do, no matter how often or vehemently he protested his innocence.

To say they didn't get along would be a gross under-statement, and Rafe took pains to avoid the man whenever possible, hence his question.

"He's delivering a rowboat he restored to some bloke in Noosa," Jane said, toeing off her sneakers and dumping her coat on her bed. "And no, I have no idea when he'll be back. Why?"

"No reason."

Rafe moved behind her and slid his hands over her hips, pulling her back so her arse cradled his erection. She moaned her approval, and he could hear her smile in the sound.

Her hair was pulled back in a ponytail, making it a simple thing to press his lips to her skin and plant a line of kisses along the smooth column of her neck and around the shell of her ear.

She moaned again and tilted her head to the side, giving him greater access. "What are you doing?"

Kissing turned to nibbling as Rafe retraced the path with his teeth, his tongue. Sliding his hands under her T-shirt, he cupped her breasts and gently tugged her nipples through the sheer fabric of her camisole.

"What do you think I'm doing?"

"I think you're trying to win Charlie's stupid bet by making me so damn horny I'll agree to just about anything to get laid. Even marry you."

Rafe's grin was unrepentant. "Is it working?" he whispered in her ear before sinking his teeth into her earlobe.

"No," she said, half laughing and slapping at his hands until he released her. Then she spun around to face him, her chin tilted up, her air superior. "Not even remotely."

"Liar," he said, his grin spreading wider.

Anchoring her hands on her hips, her humour vanished and she huffed out an irritated sigh. "Why do you do that? Why do you always assume I'm lying about this stuff?"

"I don't assume anything," he said. "I know."

"Fine. How do you *know*, then?"

"One, I've known you literally your entire life. Two, I wouldn't be very good at my job if I couldn't spot a liar at ten paces. And three, when you're turned on, as in 'super horny want to rip my clothes off and have your wicked way with me' turned on"—he grinned—"your ears turn bright red."

"They do not," she said, her voice suddenly two octaves higher. She folded her arms across her chest, but he could see her mind working, see her gaze dart to the door and back, wondering if what he'd just said was true.

He nodded towards the bathroom. "Go on. Go take a look. I'll wait."

When Jane returned a few minutes later, she did not look happy. "I really hate you right now."

His eyes widened. "Why?"

"Because I'm horny," she snapped, pointing at her bright red ears. "*All* the time! And I'm pregnant and my hormones are all out of whack and I feel like I'm going crazy. I have no life, I don't have a job, I'm broke, and I'm going to get really, really fat." She stared up at him with such a miserable expression he couldn't help but pull her into his arms and absorb her distress, to comfort her, protect her. "And my ears are red," she grumbled before smooshing her face against his body and mumbling into his chest, "And I want chocolate."

Rafe freed Jane's hair from her ponytail and gently ran his fingers through it, petting her in a way he knew she liked. Then he scooped her up, placed her on her bed and sat beside her with his back against the headboard. When she rested her head on his chest, he continued stroking her hair, and he smiled when she loosely draped her arm over his stomach and entwined one leg with his.

He knew what she was after.

Reassurance.

A voice of reason to help settle her fears and tell her everything was going to be okay. Not that she ever outright asked him for comfort, but he knew the signs. And he could do that for her. He'd been doing that for her ever since she was a little girl, always ready with a hug when she needed one. Or to tell her off when she needed that too.

The list she'd just spewed out required a bit of both.

"Let's break that down, shall we?" he said.

Jane didn't respond right away, but eventually she nodded, rubbing her cheek against his chest.

He dropped a kiss on the top of her head, then continued. "Okay, here we go. Pregnant women don't get fat, they just get more pregnant. You *do* have a job, just maybe not the one you want right now. You also have a life, one that's filled with family and friends who love you and want to help you, if only you'd stop being so bloody stubborn and let them. Yes, you're broke, but again, family, friends, love you, don't be stubborn. If you want chocolate, I will get you chocolate, and if you're really that horny, I will happily go down on you again or finger-fuck you or both. If you want me to."

"It's not the same," she mumbled quietly. "Don't get me wrong, all of those options are nice. Nicer than nice. But I want your cock. I *need* your cock. I need to feel how I feel when you fuck me. I need...." She made an exasperated sound.

Keeping his voice soft and low, he said, "What do you need, Janie? Tell me."

"I need you inside me," she said, clambering to her knees and turning to face him. "I need to feel the way I feel when you're inside me and you look at me the way you do and I feel cherished and adored and turned way the fuck on because when you screw me, it's like nothing I've ever felt with anyone but you."

She took a breath and squared her shoulders, lifted her chin and pinned him with the uncompromising stare he admired her for.

"You wanted to know why I always came to you after I ended it with someone else. Well it's because no one else ever made me feel as alive as you do. When you fuck me it feels like my whole being wants to shatter apart in ecstasy, and when you make me come with your cock, it does. I don't just see stars when you make me come, I see whole freaking galaxies, because you know what I like and what I love and no one touches me like you, no one knows my body the way *you* do. And when it's all over, I know I can lie in your arms and be surrounded by your warmth and your strength and it silences my mind. It calms me. I feel safe. Rafe, fucking you feels amazing because it's not just sex. And I know I'm being selfish, and I know you're well within your rights to tell me to piss off, but after everything that's happened, I want to feel amazing again. I need to. Please, Rafe. Please fuck me."

Wow.

Jane knelt on the bed, her hands clenched on her knees as she stared at him, waiting for him to say something, anything, but Rafe had no response. He could think of nothing to say except, "Wow."

An instant later, a barrage of questions assaulted his bewildered brain, and he didn't know which to ask first.

Whole fucking galaxies? Really?

Her boyfriends didn't cherish her? Arseholes.

And *What did she mean when she said 'it's not just sex'?*

Quickly followed by *Or... is this all a cunning ploy to win Charlie's bet?*

But before he could voice any or all of his questions, she pushed up off the bed and stalked away from him, then threw her hands in the air and said, "God, I am such a loser."

"Jane," Rafe growled, imbuing his voice with an authoritative tone. She turned to look at him and he hated the wariness he saw in her gaze, in her stance.

Jane was never wary.

She was a warrior queen who lived life by her own rules, and she didn't shy away from her emotions. She was never defeatist.

"Come here," he commanded, moving to sit on the edge of the bed, then reached out his hand and waited patiently until she took it.

"Rafe—"

"Now, Jane."

She rolled her lips between her teeth and stared at his outstretched hand for what felt like an eternity, then placed her hand in his and allowed him to pull her close, positioning her between his spread knees.

He anchored his hands on her hips, a smile tugging at his mouth when she tunnelled her fingers through his hair and stroked down the back of his neck. He loved the feel of her hands on his body, loved the little electric zing he felt where her fingertips touched his skin.

"Tell me why you think you're a loser."

"You mean besides all the reasons previously listed?" she said, staring down at him like he was dense.

Rafe smirked. "Yes, besides those reasons."

"Okay, how about the fact I seem to have turned into a raging nympho who can't get laid no matter how much I beg for it?" She fisted her hands in his hair and yanked his head back. "Why won't you fuck me?"

He shrugged. "Why won't you marry me?"

"Oh for heaven's sake, Rafe. Will you please be serious?"

"I am being serious," he said, tightening his grip on her hips when she tried to pull away from him. "Listen to me, Janie. You agree to marry me, and I swear to you it'll be on like Donkey Kong. I will go down on you morning, noon and night. I will fuck your sweet pussy six ways come Sunday, and I will give you more pleasure than you know what to do with. I promise you, beautiful, you'll be seeing galaxies for days. But until you agree to marry me, my dick stays in my pants." Jane's head dropped back until she stared at the ceiling then let out a long suffering groan, so Rafe added, "And you know what? For someone who said my dick isn't that spectacular, you sure did wax lyrical about it."

Fury flashed in her emerald greens and indignation bloomed on her cheeks. "Well do *you* know what? You suck at marriage proposals," Jane said, arms akimbo and chest heaving.

"Oh really?" This he had to hear.

"Yes, really. Stringing the words 'marry me' together makes them a proposal about as much as tossing eggs and flour in a bowl makes them a cake. Where's the sugar, Rafe? Where's the heat? You can't just plonk a goopy, powdery mess on a plate and pretend it's something it's not. I want my goddamn cake."

Something flared to life in Rafe's chest, a spark of an idea, an ember of hope. Was she saying what he thought she was saying? Did she even realise what she'd said?

He slid his hands around her and cupped her arse, pulled her closer. "Wait a sec. Are you telling me that if I propose to you properly, you'll marry me?"

Rafe watched her like a hawk, watched for all of her usual tells, her body language, her subtle ticks, and when she threw attitude at him and said, "No," he grinned like a fool.

"Liar."

Chapter Ten

R afe leaned his forearm on the shower wall and closed his eyes, visions of Jane's perfect breasts and wet pussy filling his mind as he stroked his rock-hard cock.

That afternoon, Jane had agreed to let him take the edge off her need and finger-fuck her sweet cunt, but just as he'd unzipped her jeans, her dad had come home and Rafe had thought it prudent to leave.

His dick had been as hard as granite ever since, and taking matters into his own hands had become necessary.

Taking his time, he worked himself up, wanting his orgasm and the feeling of total bliss that accompanied it to last as long as possible. He altered his speed and grip—fast and loose, slow and tight—and his head fell forwards as he felt the telltale signs of impending ecstasy grip the base of his spine and work its way towards his balls—

"Rafe?" Oliver banged on the bathroom door.

Rafe growled through gritted teeth and tried to ignore him.

Almost there... wet pussy, tight, warm, pink—

"Come on, Rafe." Oliver banged on the door again.

"Fuck off!" Rafe yelled back, then groaned with disappointment as one of the most unsatisfying orgasms of his existence spilled from his cock and was quickly washed down the drain.

Flicking off the taps with more force than necessary, he didn't even bother to wrap a towel around his hips before yanking the bathroom door open and barking at his brother. "What?"

Grinning from ear to ear as he took in Rafe's nakedness and pissed-off expression, Ollie said, "Did I interrupt something?"

Teeth clenched, Rafe ground out his reply. "I'm going to kill you. Slowly. Painfully."

"You can try," Ollie chuckled. "Shorty."

"What do you want, Ollie?"

"For you to hurry up and get your arse out of the shower before you use up all the hot water. I have a date tonight."

Rafe blew out a breath and grabbed a towel, then stepped aside for his brother to enter. "You know there are two other bathrooms you could have used?" Wrapping the towel around his hips, he grabbed his toothbrush and toothpaste.

"True. But when two showers are on at once, the water pressure sucks, and you have no idea what it takes to maintain this hair," Ollie said, loosening the long blond braid that fell down his back.

Continuing to brush his teeth with one hand, Rafe held up two fingers on his other hand and imitated scissors cutting.

"Not fucking likely, bro. A man's hair is sacred."

Rafe smirked around his toothbrush, knowing exactly how he'd get his revenge the next time Ollie pissed him off.

"So, why were you wanking?" his brother asked as he peeled off his jeans and T-shirt and climbed in the shower. "I thought you and Janie were bumping uglies again."

Rafe spit toothpaste into the sink and rinsed his mouth out. "We're not 'bumping uglies', you crass arsehole."

"Well you're definitely doing something. We all heard Jane last night. And this morning. The walls aren't exactly thick in this house, bro."

"Fuck," Rafe muttered and scrubbed his hands over his head, then leaned back against the vanity. He needed to talk to someone about this, and Ollie was as good a man as any. And his tendency to be blunt with his siblings could be in Rafe's favour. "Jane wants to have sex but I'm... hesitant."

"Why?"

"Because I don't want things to go back to the way they were between us. I want a real relationship with her this time. Not just sex."

"I get that," Oliver said, shrugging. "You still love her."

Rafe *tsked*. "Why does everyone keep saying that?"

Ollie barked a laugh. "Because if you didn't love her, you wouldn't be so insistent about her marrying you."

"I'm doing that for the baby," he said, scowling.

"I thought you were only doing that if the baby wasn't yours. Last I checked, you don't know if the baby is yours or not, yet you're insisting she marry you either way. That doesn't sound like something a man not in love would do."

Exhaling sharply, Rafe folded his arms over his chest again. "You don't understand."

"You're right, I don't. You have a gorgeous woman throwing herself at you, begging you to fuck her, and you're *not* hitting that? Tell me why, Rafe. What's the real reason? I mean, are you afraid to be happy? What?"

"Because I'm tired of Jane using me as her rebound lay,"

Rafe snapped. "If she wants to fuck me, fine. I'll fuck her 'til she can't walk straight. All I'm asking for is some commitment first. Why is that such a bad thing?"

"It's not. But there's commitment and then there's marriage. And if you're serious about making this work with her in the long term, you're going to have to compromise. Relationships aren't all or nothing, Rafe. And if you don't start taking care of her needs, she'll find someone else who will."

A spike of anger ripped through Rafe at the thought of another man touching Jane, especially now. He glared at his younger brother as Ollie stepped out of the shower, the memory of Jane's earlier outburst still fresh in his mind. "Well maybe if all she wants is my dick, I'm better off without her."

Oliver smacked Rafe upside his head.

"What was that for?" He straightened, getting ready for the inevitable fight coming his way.

"You know something, *big* brother? For a really smart guy, you can be so fucking dumb."

"You've never had a serious relationship in your entire life, so what the hell do you know about anything?"

"Just because I'm not relationship material doesn't mean I don't have friends who are, dipshit. You'd be surprised what you can learn about things if you actually bother to ask questions."

"Well that was cryptic. Thanks for that."

Ollie shook his head, shoved his way past Rafe and yanked the bathroom door open. "Like I said. Fucking dumb."

Then he disappeared down the hall and into his bedroom, slamming the door behind him, and leaving Rafe even more confused than he had been a moment ago.

Rafe lay in bed, staring at the ceiling, his mind a whirlwind of thought.

Did Oliver have a point about marrying Jane? Was Rafe expecting too much? Not compromising enough? Initially, yes, he'd asked her to marry him because of the baby, to ensure he could protect the child if Sam—or anyone else, for that matter—came looking to make life difficult for them. But somewhere in all the back and forth, he'd realised he wasn't as altruistic as he thought.

He wanted her. Plain and simple.

But was his fear of repeating their past keeping them from moving forwards?

Scrubbing a hand over his face, he muttered, "Fuck."

He punched his pillow and tried getting comfortable, but every time he closed his eyes, all he saw was Jane, uncertainty swimming in her clear green gaze. And all he heard was the slight tremor in her lovely voice as she spilled her reasons for using him for so many years.

Galactic orgasms and a feeling of safety.

Taking a deep breath, he slowly let it out again. He supposed there could have been worse reasons for her to use him the way she had. He couldn't think of any right at that moment, but he was sure they existed. But it still didn't explain why she'd always left him afterwards.

Obviously he hadn't made her feel *that* safe.

"Maybe I should go see her," he said, then nodded, his mind made up. "I'm going to go see her."

But before he could even swing his legs over the edge of the bed, he heard the familiar sound of timber and glass rattling and sliding, and then a soft feminine grunting preceded his view of a very nice, round, denim-clad arse.

"Speak of the devil," he muttered, shaking his head as he watched her emerge through the window. "Making this a nightly thing, are we?"

Blowing her hair out of her face, Jane turned to Rafe and said, "What thing?"

"You, breaking and entering into my room in the middle of the night."

Ignoring his bemused expression, she began explaining why she'd come, and it didn't appear to be for the same reason as the previous night.

"I have a problem," she said, her tone almost busi-nesslike.

A hole opened up inside Rafe and his stomach fell in. Was Ollie right? Had Jane found someone else to satisfy her needs?

His gut tightened with self-reproach, with anger and jealousy.

She's mine.

Shoving his emotions down, Rafe snorted. "That's one word for it," he said, moving off the bed and holding her steady while helping her unhook her shoelace from the window latch. "You do know no one will think less of you for using the front door, right? Has to be easier than trying to cram your pregnant arse through my window every night."

Her hand dropped to her belly and she scowled at him. "Door-schmoor. I'm perfectly capable of breaking and entering well into my second trimester, thank you very much." She shrugged out of her coat and removed her shoes. "Now, do you want to hear about my problem... or not?" she said.

Her speech staggered and Rafe's tension eased some-what when he noticed Jane's gaze had snagged on his naked chest. She licked her lips, rubbed her hand across the base of her throat and swallowed hard.

Not the actions of a sexually satisfied woman.

He bit back a grin and hid his relief. *Fucking Ollie messing with my head.* "Hit me with it. What's happened between when I left you to have your nap and now?"

Dragging her gaze up to meet his, she planted one hand on her hip and said, "Do you mean when you promised me sexual satisfaction then chickened out and left me hanging?"

Rafe scowled. "I didn't chicken out. Alec came home. And I was not going to fool around with you within ear shot of your father." He shifted uncomfortably. "He hates me enough as it is."

Shaking her head, Jane said, "What is it with you two? Honestly, I don't—"

"You said you had a problem?" Rafe cut her off, reminded her why she'd come. The last thing he wanted to discuss with her was the reason behind his complicated relationship with her father. He'd made a promise. He intended to keep it.

No matter how much he hated doing so.

Now it was Jane's turn to scowl, unimpressed by Rafe's sudden change in subject. "Yes," she said. "I got an email from the man who outfitted my food truck saying it's ready to be picked up and requesting the next payment." Pulling her phone from her pocket, she opened the message. "Can you take a look? Tell me if it's real or not?"

Taking the phone from her outstretched hand, Rafe switched into work mode and all emotion deserted him as he read through the email. Jane paced across the room, wringing her hands and throwing anxious looks his way every few seconds.

It was very distracting.

"Sit down, Jane," he said, pointing at the bed.

She sat immediately, but as soon as she did, her leg started bouncing uncontrollably, which was even more distracting than watching her pace back and forth.

Rafe sat beside her on the bed and indicated for her to swing her legs over his lap, then rubbed them with one hand while scrolling through the message with the other.

Eventually he looked at her. "The email looks legitimate," he said, then frowned. "You've actually seen this truck with your own eyes, yes?"

She nodded. "Yes."

"In person, not just in photographs or online?"

"Yes, I've seen it in person. Geez, Rafe, I'm not a total moron. I went to Melbourne with Sam to meet the outfitter, Mr Bridges. He liked my pecan pie. We had a meeting about my business and how I wanted the van painted, what equipment I wanted installed. We even discussed the permits I needed."

"Okay. Good."

"No, Rafe, not good. After everything else that's happened, I'd assumed the truck was a scam too, just another elaborate prop to sell Sam's lies. And I figured the outfitter was probably one of his arsehole mates or an actor or something, but if it's real, I'm screwed."

"How so?"

Jane toyed with the hem of her shirt, twisted it around her fingers again and again. A sure sign she was more upset than she wanted to let on. "I wanted to buy the truck outright. Just do it, done. It was in my budget to do so, and besides general maintenance, it would have been one less thing to worry about. But Sam convinced me to lease the truck instead, because it meant I had more capital sitting in the bank and I could afford better advertising and hire an assistant sooner rather than later. Of course now I realise he just didn't want me spending the money because it meant there'd be less for him to steal."

"But it also means you're stuck paying off a lease, and will probably end up paying out even more money than if you'd just bought the bloody truck in the first place," Rafe concluded with a heavy sigh and shake of his head.

He hated leases for that exact reason and avoided them like the plague. They were also notoriously hard to get out of and generally came with a laundry list of hidden fees and charges.

"That fucking little shitstain."

She looked up at him imploringly. "What do I do?"

Rafe reached out and tucked a lock of her hair behind her ear, his touch lingering in the silky soft strands. "Forward me copies of the email and the lease and leave it with me. I'll see what I can find out tomorrow, okay?"

"Okay." Blowing out a sigh of relief, the tension in her body visibly eased and a small smile pulled at her mouth. "Thank you, Rafe."

"No thanks necessary, Janie. I told you the other day, if you need *anything*, just ask," he said, handing back her phone. "Now is that the only thing you came over to discuss, or do you *need* something else?"

If her sudden grin was anything to go by, Jane caught the meaning behind his question. "Well, it is night-time," she hedged. "And you did promise. And since you weren't able to—*ahem*—lend me a hand this afternoon, I'll admit to being a wee bit antsy."

Wrapping his arms around her, he pulled her into his lap, then positioned her so she was straddling him. Lowering his mouth to her throat, he growled, "The only thing that got me through that shit-ton of paperwork this morning, was thinking about my tongue in your pussy and how good it felt with your thighs locked around my head when you came."

"Is that a fact?" Jane chuckled, wriggling closer. "And to think the good citizens of Melville's Cross call you 'the boring bastard'."

He raised a brow and grinned. "They think I'm boring, do they?"

"Yep. Everyone thinks you're this uptight, straight-laced prig of a man. Oh, if only they knew you the way I do," she said, walking her fingers down his chest towards the waistband of his pyjama bottoms. "A domineering, dirty-talking, rough-fucking *tease* who loves eating pussy."

Ignoring her "tease" comment, he grabbed her wrists and restrained them behind her back, thrusting her chest forwards. Sucking his lower lip between his teeth, he let his gaze wander slowly over her firm tits and down to the apex of her thighs where it pushed against his straining cock.

"Not just eating it, beautiful. Fucking it. Saying it. Pussy. And cunt. I fucking love the word cunt."

Jane laughed again. "You have such a dirty mouth," she said, shaking her head at him.

"And lucky for you I know just how to use it." He took the neckline of her shirt in his teeth and pulled on it, let it go and watched it snap back. "Take this off. Take it all off. I have an idea."

He loved how easily she obeyed him, how quickly she slipped from his lap and stripped out of her clothes.

So confident.

And why wouldn't she be? She was gorgeous.

She arched one brow. "Oh?"

Rafe stood as he watched her, and once she was naked,

he slid his hands around her hips and pulled her into his embrace. Her skin felt so soft and warm beneath his palms, and he let his gaze drift over her lithe little body.

It never ceased to amaze him how beautiful she was, how much her subtle curves turned him on, or how deceptively soft she was for such a small woman, how much her body wiggled and jiggled when he smacked her arse, or when he ploughed into her from behind.

And he adored the way her small breasts fit so perfectly in his palms, how her dark red nipples hardened against his tongue. How she moaned so softly when he took those nipples into his mouth and laved them with attention.

He licked his lips. Soon. He'd taste them again soon.

But for now....

"How about you sit on my face and let me take you for a ride?"

"What?" Pink spots bloomed on her cheeks as embarrassment engulfed her. She tried to pull away, but he tightened his arms around her. "No! I'm heavier than the last time we did it that way." She looked away, avoiding his gaze and ran her hand over her slightly swollen belly. "I might, you know, suffocate you."

Rafe hooked a knuckle under her chin and lifted her face to his. "Then I'll die a happy man."

She pursed her lips. "You're incorrigible."

Rafe squeezed her arse in one big hand. "I think you mean irresistible," he said, then slapped her bottom just hard enough to make her gasp.

"That too," she conceded quietly, slipping her arms around his waist and staring up at him with her beautiful green gaze. And not for the first time he realised he'd happily drown in those eyes, in their warmth and affection and—

Love?

Did Jane still love him?

There was one way to test the waters. He smiled and stroked her hair. "Will you marry me?" he whispered.

Jane looked taken aback by the change in conversational direction, or possibly just because he'd phrased it as a question that time instead of his usual demand.

I am trying, beautiful.

It took her a few seconds to answer him, which gave him hope that he hadn't been wrong when he'd guessed she would say yes to him eventually.

As soon as he nailed the proposal.

And his hope did a double take when Jane didn't outright refuse him as she had been doing but said instead, "Get on the bed."

Chapter Eleven

"**G**ood morning, beautiful," Rafe murmured in Jane's ear. Then slowly kissed a path down her neck and across her shoulder.

Jane groaned her disapproval at the sound of his alarm going off, then rolled over and glared up at him, her lips twisted in annoyance. "Good morning," she grumbled. "Please make it stop."

Rafe's warm, sleep-roughened chuckle met her ears as the blaring from his old clock radio morphed into quiet easy listening music on whatever old-people station he had it tuned to.

"What happened to 'I'm a baker'?"

"What happened was someone kept me up all night," she grumbled, punching her pillow. "And I'm sleeping for two."

Not that she'd minded staying up at the time. Jane had finally conceded to Rafe's demands that she take his tongue for a ride, mostly because with her ever expanding weight and waistline she didn't think she'd have many more opportunities to do so. Then after said tongue lashing he'd given her a full-body massage with lavender-infused body oil because he said he'd read a bunch of articles about pregnancy causing insomnia.

By the time he'd finished pampering her, she'd been so relaxed she hadn't noticed it was one o'clock in the morning.

Rafe chuckled again and pushed his morning wood against her arse, the layers of their pyjamas between them doing nothing to lessen her body's instant reaction to the contact. She squirmed, her pussy growing wet in eagerness for a cock she wasn't getting anytime soon.

Stubborn tease of a bastard.

Her mood instantly improved when he traced the pad of his thumb over her bottom lip and asked, "Can I kiss your mouth yet?"

Sucking his thumb into her mouth and nipping him with her teeth, she replied, "Have you abandoned your silly plan to marry me yet?"

"Silly?" He scowled down at her. "I'll show you silly, woman." And the next thing she knew, his big body was pinning her down so she couldn't move and his fingers were digging into her ribs, tickling her ruthlessly. "Who's silly now, huh?" he said amid her laughter and cries for mercy.

"Okay, okay, I give. You win."

Rafe eased up on the tickling and stroked his hands over her body instead. It always felt good when he touched her like that, as though he couldn't get enough of her, needed more of her. As if she were his favourite toy and he couldn't wait to play with her.

Her already horny hormones kicked it up a level.

"What do I win?" he asked, smiling down at her with that intensely wicked grin he reserved just for her.

She narrowed her eyes, cocked one brow and spoke with mock suspicion. "What do you want?"

Tugging down the front of her camisole, he latched his lips around her nipple and gave it a gentle suck—*oh dear Lord, that feels amazing*—and she suddenly realised why women were willing to put themselves through pregnancy over and over again. Every erogenous zone on her body had been dialled up to 1,000, and her brain turned to mush at even the slightest provocation.

Lips? Tongue? Big burly man-hands with long, thick, probing fingers that knew exactly what they were looking for and found it every damn time? *Oh yeah.* It was all good.

Really, *really* good.

And it certainly explained why she'd turned into a raging sex fiend. Even her morning sickness seemed to have taken a back seat to her libido since Rafe came back into her life.

Huh.

"How about you take a shower with me after my run? Let me wash your hair."

"Wash my hair, huh?" she said, ignoring her sudden realisation about Rafe and letting her laughter bubble up from within her at his odd request. "Is that what the kids are calling it these days?"

Rafe laughed and pulled away. "Cheeky."

As he moved around the room getting ready for his morning jog, Jane realised—and not for the first time—she could quite happily watch Rafael Bennett all day long and never get bored.

Rafe was a physically stunning man, and the way he moved was effortlessly graceful. Shorter than his brothers by a few inches, but leaner too, his shoulders were broad, his hips narrow, his abs defined and his biceps impressive.

No one would ever look at Rafe and mistake him for anything other than what he was.

Strong.

Disciplined.

The hair on his chest was soft and springy and covered little more than his pecs, but more hair grew below his waist. A sexy trail tapered out from his navel, widening to cover his lower abdomen and encircle his gorgeous cock.

Jane sucked her bottom lip between her teeth and let her gaze linger on the front of his running shorts. If he thought she'd "waxed lyrical" about his dick the day before, it was nothing compared to everything she hadn't said.

Jesus but she loved his cock.

It truly was the most perfect dick she'd ever seen, and she'd seen her fair share over the years. Not as many as some but, you know, a few.

She just wished she had someone she could talk to about it, compare sizes and boast about it, but when your BFF was your lover's little sister, it pretty much guaranteed all conversations about sex and penis size were shoved in the TMI basket to be forever ignored and eventually forgotten.

Sighing quietly, she dragged her gaze away from his crotch and let it settle on his insanely handsome face. Rafe had the face of an angel.

A fallen angel, to be sure, but weren't they the best kind?

With his dark, soulful eyes and sinfully decadent lips, he drew attention from the ladies wherever he went. Add to that a sharp mind and sharper wit and he really was the whole package.

Good looks, strength, intelligence.

Rafe could have his pick of women and he knew it.

So what the hell does he see in me?

She knew he found her attractive even with her ginger-blonde hair, freckled face and tiny tits. They'd never had an issue where sex was concerned.

No, their differences manifested elsewhere.

Rafe was quiet, contemplative, studious and in a life-long commitment to common sense. Jane was... none of those things. She was brash, even arrogant, and often lacked the ability to keep her thoughts and feelings to herself, as she'd proven the previous afternoon in her bedroom when she'd spewed her insecurities all over the poor man. The man who'd then said her name in that bossy tone of voice she loved, pulled her into his arms and made everything better.

Almost everything.

The man who, for some inexplicable reason, was insisting on marrying her.

Before having sex.

Weirdo.

"So, what are you doing today?"

He glanced her way with a raised brow. "Finally finished eye-banging me, have you?"

Her cheeks heated and she ducked her head. "What? No."

"No, you weren't eye-banging me, or no, you're not finished?" He grinned, and Jane, remembering what he'd told her the day before, immediately covered her ears. Rafe laughed out loud. "That's not how I know."

Staring up at him with narrowed eyes, she asked, "Then how did you know I was watching you? You were getting dressed. I could have been sleeping for all you know. You weren't paying me any attention at all."

Crowding her until she flopped back on the bed, he crawled over the top of her and pinned her down with his big body, his knees either side of her thighs, her wrists gripped in his powerful hands. He whispered in her ear, "That's where you're wrong, Janie. I always know when you're watching me, because I'm *always* watching you."

Her heart beat faster. His words, his tone sounded so deliciously possessive. A shiver of excitement ran through her and her breath shuddered out of her lungs.

But then he pulled back and set her free, and she missed his closeness, his heat. "But to answer your question," he continued, sitting on the edge of the bed and pulling on his sneakers, "we have an appointment for the paternity test at the GP clinic at nine, and then I have to get to the office. I've organised for a couple of the part-time legal secretaries we hired at the firm in Brisbane to help me sort through the shit-fight I inherited from the previous counsel. What about you?"

Jane pulled her knees up to her chest and wrapped her arms around them. "I don't know. Mum's insisting I take the week off, and until we find out more about that food truck...." She shrugged, feeling very uncertain and a little bit lost. She couldn't remember the last time she didn't have a plan.

Rafe stood up and stretched his arms over his head. His fingertips brushed the ceiling. "I'll look into the truck situation when I get to the office, and I'm sure you'll think of something to keep yourself occupied. You always do." Then he bent and kissed her cheek. "I'll be back soon."

Too awake to go back to sleep, Jane crawled out of bed and pulled on one of Rafe's man-cardigans. *Mandigans*. It was huge on her small body, big enough to use as a dressing gown, and she wrapped it tightly around herself and made her way out to the kitchen.

It was still dark outside, and she absently wondered how Rafe knew where the hell he was going on his morning runs.

There were no street lamps along Bennett's Road, and the moon offered little light.

Flicking the kitchen light on, she shuffled across the room and put the kettle on. While she waited for the water to boil, she hunted through the fridge and the pantry for something to make for breakfast.

When she grabbed a packet of bacon from the fridge, her stomach rumbled and she stilled, waiting for the nausea that usually hit around this time of morning. But it didn't come.

What did hit her was how incredibly hungry she was, and then she realised she'd barely eaten the day before.

Sweeping her hand over her stomach, she said, "Sorry, kid. You must be starving in there." Then she blew out a breath, pulled her hair up in a loose bun and got to work.

By the time Rafe returned from his run—looking far sexier than any man had a right to at that time of day—she had the kitchen table set and laid out with enough food to feed the whole household. Crispy bacon, eggs—both poached and scrambled—buttered sourdough toast, mushrooms sautéed in garlic butter, roasted cherry tomatoes, smashed avocado with a side of smoked salmon and a family-sized plunger of French roast coffee ready to pour.

Rafe stood in the middle of the kitchen, his hands anchored on his hips, his mouth hanging open as he stared at the table. "Move in with me," he said, and she grinned at the hint of awe in his rich voice.

She gently elbowed his ribs. "You only want me for my cooking."

He pulled her back against his chest and wrapped his arms around her belly, caressed her baby bump in a way that made her ovaries explode in happiness. Leaning down, he kissed her nape. "That's not the only thing I want you for," he assured her, his words vibrating over her skin, making her horny. Well, hornier. Being pinned to the bed twice but left untouched while Rafe went for his jog had made her horny.

Turning her head to the side, she breathed in his healthy male scent, then pressed her thighs together.

Licking her lips, she said, "So... cooking and because I'm pregnant?"

His body shook behind her, his soft chuckling bouncing through her. Then he slipped his hand under the mandigan and cupped her pussy through her underwear, pushed the pad of his thumb against her clit and gently rubbed. The soft rasp of lace over the tiny bundle of nerves was electric.

"Cooking." He kissed her neck. "Because you're pregnant." He nipped the curve of her ear. "And because you're the sexiest fucking woman I've ever known," he said, drawing a line over her panties and along her slit, teasing her. Anticipation threatened to buckle her knees beneath her. "You wet for me, baby?"

Teeth sinking into her bottom lip, she nodded. "Always."

"Then move in with me," he murmured quietly. Easing her panties aside, he slid his finger inside her hot, eager pussy and she had to lean against him or fall to the floor in a boneless heap. "If nothing else, it'll save you the trouble of climbing through my bedroom window every time you want me to li—"

"Do I smell bacon?"

Rafe quickly pulled away from Jane, growling his displeasure at the interruption. Wolf and Abby entered the kitchen—seemingly oblivious to the sexual frustration they were causing—followed soon after by Oliver and Ulysses.

Jane wrapped herself up tighter in what was now his favourite cardigan ever and took a seat opposite his sister.

Ducking her head, she hid her smile from the others, but Rafe caught her attention and winked, then watched her eyes glaze over with lust and need as he sucked his finger inside his mouth.

The move backfired.

Her taste exploded on his tongue and his cock sprang to life, forcing him to hastily sit before his burgeoning erection could embarrass him in front of his family.

Sitting beside Jane, Rafe dug into the feast she'd prepared and listened to his family shower his lover in compliments. Watched her wave them away as though her culinary talents were nothing at all.

But he saw the pleasure in her eyes, the pride she took in a job well done.

Reaching for the bacon, he said, "So, what do we all think about Jane moving into The Forge?"

Jane immediately began coughing as though something had gone down the wrong way. Rafe patted her on the back until she waved him off too.

"You're moving in?" Abby's eyes widened and her smile was instant. "Yes," she said to no one in particular and pumped her fist in the air.

"I haven't said yes yet," Jane said, shooting a glare at Rafe.

"You will," Abby said, reaching for the toast. She shrugged one shoulder, nonchalant, as though Jane moving in were a foregone conclusion. "You have to."

Rafe smiled at the confidence in her voice. It was a sound he hadn't heard in far too long and Rafe would be forever grateful to her fiancé, Wolf, for the gift he'd given not only his sister, but all of them.

After two abusive relationships followed by years of living in near seclusion, Abby had been resistant to the author's attempts to woo her, preferring instead to use him for sex. But love had won out eventually and Wolf had brought Abby back to them, stronger, happier.

And he didn't miss the parallels between their situation and his. That in some respects, he now faced a similar challenge with Jane.

"I have to, huh?" Jane's brow slid up and her lips twitched with amusement.

"Yes, you have to. I am seriously outnumbered now that Dad, Ollie and Rafe have moved home again. I need another woman around to help even the odds. Besides," she continued, a wistful tone sliding through her voice, "I wanna help out with my new niece."

Rafe cast a sidelong glance at Jane as she poured herself a cup of coffee. She was gnawing on her lip and avoiding Abby's gaze, and he realised what she was probably thinking: Jane was pregnant and Abby was unable to bear children. How could she deny her friend the chance to be a mother? Even if only temporarily?

His protective instincts took over and there was no indecision about who he was protecting.

Jane.

Frowning at his sister across the table, he said, "Hey. No guilt trips, Abbs. If Jane moves in, I want it to be because she wants to be here, not because she feels obligated to you or me or anyone else."

"Guilt trip?" Abby returned his frown before understanding widened her eyes with horror and her mouth fell open. He didn't even need to hear the catch in her voice when she spoke next to know he'd made a huge error in judgement. "How could you think—"

"*Liebchen*, look at me," Wolf commanded sharply, his deep voice booming in the suddenly quiet kitchen.

She stared at the table and shook her head. "I didn't mean—"

Wolf gripped her chin in one hand and squeezed her fingers with the other. Forcing her to look him in the eyes, he said, "Breathe, little nymph."

And she did.

Rafe watched his sister's anxiety ease out of her with every deep breath she took at Wolf's command, and within moments she was back to glaring at him. Along with everyone else at the table.

Her free hand clenched into a fist. "I didn't mean it like that."

Oliver shook his head at him. "Arse."

Then Jane elbowed him in the ribs, and not gently. "Apologise. Now."

His jaw tightening with self-reproach, he said, "I'm sorry, Abbs. I didn't think before I spoke." Then he blew out a breath and looked sideways at Jane.

She stared back, shaking her head, a frown pulling at her brow and mouth. "Idiot."

"Don't be too mad at him, my dears," his father weighed in. "Men will say and do all manner of foolhardy things in the quest to protect their family."

Oliver pointed his fork at him. "You've been away from home too long if you think for even a second anyone would have to protect a baby from Abby," he growled. "She'd throw herself on a live grenade to save a kid. Especially family."

"Or if you think anyone could make Jane do something

143

she doesn't want to do," Abby added, her eyes narrowed and her lip curled.

Heat crawled up Rafe's neck as he was roundly chastised. "I said I'm sorry," he ground out. "I withdraw the comment."

Jaw clenched, his sister nodded at him then turned back to her breakfast. And everyone followed suit.

After an unbearably awkward minute of nothing but the sound of eating, Ulysses asked Abby, "Why do you think the babe will be a girl?"

Abby flicked her gaze to Rafe, as though trying to gauge his mood, then lifted her chin and said, "Henry, Paul and Charlie all had girls. I figured it was a foregone conclusion."

His father harrumphed. "I figured four granddaughters was karma coming back to bite me in the arse."

Jane burst out laughing, and just like that the lingering tension eased from the room, and Rafe finally relaxed.

"I'll try my best not to add to your burden, Uly," Jane said, then lifted her coffee to her lips. "What the—" She frowned at her cup then slowly turned to glare at Rafe. "What did you do?"

Rafe grinned then took a sip of his own coffee. "It's decaf."

"Gah!" She shuddered and put her mug down. "I should have realised you were up to something when you didn't stop me from pouring myself a cup."

Everyone pushed their mugs away, except Wolf, who drank deeply from his. "What?" he said, realising he was the centre of attention.

"How can you drink that?" Ulysses asked, staring at his future son-in-law as though he'd just swallowed a live octopus.

Wolf shrugged, unconcerned. "I'm guessing you've

never drunk the coffee in a teacher's lounge at a public high school before. Believe me, decaf's an improvement."

An hour later they were sitting in the waiting room of the doctor's office, Jane flicking through month old magazines, looking at recipes, and Rafe silently noting how many people filled the other chairs.

He calculated the time it would take for the rest of the town to know Jane Melville was having his baby to be roughly as long as it took for the doctor to see them.

Already he could see the glint of mobile phone screens surreptitiously appearing in the hands of onlookers, people who glanced away with more speed than necessary when he caught their eye.

Adding fuel to the fire was Jane's decision to wear a form-fitting T-shirt. "Go big or go home," she'd said when he'd questioned her choice. "You wanted people to know. Now they will."

She was right. He did want people to know. Rafe was tired of hiding his feelings for Jane and it had occurred to him that just maybe, by forcing their budding relationship into the light of day, Jane might finally admit her true feelings too.

Not that he'd admitted his, exactly. He'd been denying them to everyone, even himself. But who was he kidding? His feelings for this woman hadn't changed in sixteen years, and try as he might to forget her, forget how she turned his world upside-down and shook the fuck out of it, he couldn't. Because in Rafe's world, filled with rules and law and responsibility, Jane was the sweetly scented summer breeze.

She was the highest point on a rollercoaster right before the stomach-flipping plunge.

She was the peas to his carrots.

Two complete opposites who fit perfectly together.

Rafe could be himself with Jane, and her him. They didn't have to hide their true natures from one another as they did from everyone else, as *he* did from everyone else. Jane was far more courageous in that department.

The boring bastard.

She was the only one outside the Bennett clan who didn't see him that way, and with any luck she'd be a Bennett soon.

At least he hoped.

He let his gaze sweep over her face, smiled at the look of concentration he saw as her gaze danced over the page and her lips moved silently as she read. Then he looked lower, lingered on her breasts for a moment before settling on her stomach.

The soft white cotton of her T-shirt clung to her body and accentuated the subtle curve of her baby bump. Confirmed the rumours that'd been swirling through town since the wedding debacle.

She was pregnant.

And his presence in the doctor's office that morning would only be seen in one light.

She was pregnant with *his* kid, not the bloke's she'd been going to marry.

"Jane? Rafe?"

Doctor Chen called their names and ushered them through the door of her office, closing it behind them. "Please, have a seat," she said, smiling as she settled herself in her own chair. "Now, what can I help you with today? Is your nausea still giving you trouble?"

"No, nothing like that," Jane assured her. "It's actually gotten better the last couple of days. I haven't thrown up since Sunday."

The keys on the doctor's computer keyboard made a click-clack sound as she took notes. "Great! And you're getting enough sleep?"

Jane glanced at Rafe and grinned. "Yeah. I've very recently had some help there."

"Oh?"

Rafe rubbed the back of his neck. "I've been giving Jane massages before bed," he said. "With lavender oil."

No way was he telling the good doctor the whole truth: that for the past two nights he'd given Jane orgasms so intense she'd practically passed out after coming all over his face, then lay curled up in his arms, softly snoring until their alarms went off in the morning.

"I see," she said, and made more notes. "That's good." She faced them again and spoke to Rafe. "When Jane came to see me, to confirm her pregnancy, she told me she thought the baby was yours. I'm happy to see you taking an active roll here. Especially after the... unpleasantness over the weekend."

"Of course," Rafe said, shifting in his seat. "But that's why we're here." He glanced at Jane, then took her hand, more for his own benefit than hers. "We need a paternity test done."

All semblance of warmth vanished, her brow shot up to her hairline and her whole face pinched in annoyance. "I see." More typing.

He threw a pleading look at Jane. "Please help."

Grinning, Jane said, "It's okay, Marie. His heart's in the right place."

Doctor Chen narrowed her gaze on Rafe again. "Oh?"

"I need to know if the baby's mine or not," he said, then told the doctor what he'd told Jane over the weekend.

By the time he'd finished explaining, her face had softened again and her typing had lost its murderous edge. "So if the baby isn't yours, you intend to adopt it?" She shook her head. "I did not see that coming. Usually when men want a paternity test, it's to get out of paying child support."

The printer on her desk whirred to life and a few seconds later she was scrawling her signature across the bottom of the printout and handing it to Jane.

"Take this next door to pathology. All we need is blood sample from you, and a cheek swab from Rafe, then they'll send it to Brisbane for analysis and I'll give you a call when we get the results back."

"When should that be?" Jane asked.

"This time next week. These sorts of tests are pretty straightforward."

The visit to pathology took less than ten minutes, and then they were off to Rafe's office. He'd offered to drive Jane home but she'd asked if she could stay with him instead.

He was happy to keep her close by. It would give him more time to work on his marriage sales pitch. But he warned her anyway, "You'll be bored."

"Nope. You were right. I thought of something to do."

"Yeah?"

"I'm going to write a cook book," she'd said, flashing him a smile a mile wide.

Rafe smiled back. "That's my girl."

As he parked his car on the street out front, he saw two women dressed in office attire standing by the door. His hired help. One of them had her hands cupped around her face as she peered through the window into what would be his reception area.

The other was Donna, his former assistant at the firm in Brisbane.

Jane glared in the other woman's direction. "What is *she* doing here?"

"I have no idea," Rafe said, a lead weight settling in his stomach.

His ex-assistant was not a Jane fan and vice versa. He'd rarely spoken to either of them about the other but knew they'd butted heads a few times over the years when Jane had visited his office in the city. Whenever he'd asked what their beef was about, he got the standard reply of "She's rude" or "She just rubs me the wrong way".

But he could read between the lines.

Both women were fiercely protective of those they considered their own, and they'd both staked a claim on him.

"I requested two junior secretaries. Part-timers."

Jane made an annoyed sound that was half scoff, half growl. "I always suspected she had a thing for you," she said, unfastening her seatbelt.

"She's married," Rafe said, fighting back a grin as he turned to face her.

She lifted one shoulder. "So?"

"To another woman."

Eyes widening in understanding, she exhaled and her body deflated, her argument rendered invalid. "Oh."

He wrapped his hand around her nape and pulled her closer, then bringing his mouth within a hair's breadth of hers, he whispered, "Are you jealous, baby?" Jane sucked in a breath and Rafe felt her lips quiver gently against his, felt her return his grin.

"Don't be absurd," she whispered back. "You know I'm not into chicks."

Only Jane could put him in his place and make him laugh while doing it.

After a quick round of introductions, Rafe praised the powers-that-be that Donna had hijacked the work request to be there. After working together for six years, she knew how he operated and what he liked and was confident she'd have the place straightened out by the weekend.

Unfortunately, they'd also long ago reached that point in their working relationship where she felt free to speak her mind without fear of censure.

Rafe had just gotten off the phone, investigating Jane's food truck mess and making follow-up arrangements, when his ex-assistant dropped a box of files on the edge of his desk then stood, arms akimbo, frowning at him.

"What?" he said, busying himself with the next job on his to-do list. He had a good idea what she was going to say and braced himself for a lecture.

"She's pregnant?" He didn't answer her. He didn't need to. "Is it yours?"

He flicked his gaze to hers then back to his work. "We believe so."

"You *believe* so? So you're not sure?"

Rafe exhaled sharply and gave her his full attention. "Is there a point to this?"

Her stance lost some of its cockiness and her face softened. "Look, from the little you've told me over the years and from what I've seen, it's not hard to guess you two have a long and complicated history, but I've also known you long enough to know how you are whenever she shows up in your life. And more importantly, how you are when she disappears again. And now there's a baby thrown in the mix for good measure. A baby she *claims* is yours."

Brow pinching in a tight frown, Rafe suddenly realised how much he hated how that sounded.

A baby she claims is yours.

He wanted the baby to be his. No. The baby *was* his. Whether he was the biological father or not, Jane's baby was *his* child.

Donna sighed quietly. "You're a good man, Rafe. But if your mood over the last three months is anything to go by, your last encounter with this woman was no picnic. I don't want to see you get hurt again."

Knowing he had friends like Donna looking out for him, Rafe smiled. "Thank you," he said. "I appreciate your concern. But Jane's not going anywhere this time, and neither am I." At Donna's unconvinced stare, he added, "I'm going to marry that woman."

Her frown deepened and she thumbed over her shoulder at the reception area where Jane was working on her book. "Wasn't she left at the altar three days ago?"

Rafe grinned. "Like you said, long and complicated." Then he gave Donna a set of office keys and a list of instructions. "I'll be back Friday arvo at the latest."

"Wait, what? Where are you going?"

"Melbourne."

"And what will you be doing in Melbourne?"

Grin widening, he rubbed his hands together. "Hopefully, winning a bet."

Chapter Twelve

Jane tapped her foot impatiently. The early morning drizzle made for a miserable winter's day as they waited for Mr Bridges, the food truck outfitter, to arrive and open his shop.

"It's nearly spring," she grumbled to Rafe, standing beside her with his hands shoved in his pockets, "Why the hell is it so cold?"

The big man shrugged. "It's Melbourne," he said, frowning down at her. "Are you warm enough?"

"Not really." Shivering, she tugged her coat tighter around herself. It didn't help.

"Here." Rafe pulled her close against his body, instructed her to slip her arms under his jacket and around his waist then wrapped his coat around her back, cocooning her in warmth. Snuggling closer, she made a sound of contentment. Rafe chuckled and rested his cheek against the top of her head, rubbed his big hands up and down her back. "Better?"

Jane smiled. "Much," she said, stifling a yawn.

"Good."

They didn't talk much after that, just held each other as they tried to stay warm and dry under the inadequate overhang outside the warehouse style workshop.

The previous day when Rafe had said they were flying to Melbourne, she'd thought he'd been joking. But an hour later Wolf and Abby were driving them to the Sunshine Coast Airport, and a few hours after that they were checking into the QT, one of the swankiest hotels in town, smack dab in the middle of the highly coveted theatre district.

Last minute business-class plane tickets and a room in a five star hotel.

It would have cost him a small fortune.

On the flight, Rafe had filled her in about what they were doing, said he'd spoken to Mr Bridges and explained the situation, but unfortunately the lease was airtight and legally binding. Then he'd offered to pay out the lease and she'd almost thrown up on him.

Thankfully she could still blame the nausea on the baby and not have to admit to the stomach churning anxiety eating away at her from the inside out.

And the cause of her anxiety?

Rafe's overwhelming generosity.

She'd started a running tally of everything Rafe had done for her and calculated it would take her approximately the rest of her life to pay him back, which, considering he still wanted to marry her, she guessed he was okay with.

Especially since he'd popped the question twice since leaving Melville's Cross. Once on the plane when he'd leaned in and whispered in her ear, bit her earlobe and made her blush three shades of red when the flight attendant caught Rafe with his hand on Jane's boob, and then again at dinner.

She'd been impressed he'd worded it as a question both times, that he'd seemingly progressed from his simple demand of "marry me".

At dinner, he'd even looked like he was going to get down on one knee, until she'd threatened to cut him if he did. The last thing she wanted to do was say "yes" simply because they were in the middle of a busy restaurant and she was embarrassed. And she knew instinctively she would have said "yes" because the only thing more mortifying would have been publically shaming Rafe by saying "no".

She cared for him too deeply to ever do that.

After dinner they'd gone for a stroll and stopped by a little gelato place she'd discovered years ago. She was happy to find it was right where she'd left it. Although, for an ice cream joint she'd felt ridiculously underdressed—and more than a little travel-worn—in the same blue jeans and T-shirt she'd worn all day.

The fact she'd added her favourite leather jacket and a cute pair of boots for their dinner date hadn't relieved her feeling of inadequacy, considering they'd been surrounded by theatre goers dressed to the nines in designer outfits.

Jane had never really cared about clothes before—a fashion mogul she was not—but standing in a gelato shop surrounded by such wealth only further illustrated the great divide between what she'd had a week ago, and what she had at that moment.

A week ago she'd been a financially independent business owner. Now she felt like a mooch veering dangerously close into gold-digger territory, and the acid burn of failure was beginning to eat a hole in her stomach.

But what was she supposed to do? Say "No thanks, Rafe, I'd much rather drown in sea of debt than suck it up and accept your help".

She had her pride but she wasn't completely stupid. Besides, even if she refused, the stubborn man would probably just do it anyway.

"What are you thinking about?" Rafe murmured against her hair.

Jane sighed quietly. "Last night."

Rafe cupped her arse and squeezed. "Me too." And she knew *exactly* what he was thinking about.

When they'd returned from their walk, they'd showered together in their luxury bathroom. It had been torture.

Deliciously erotic torture.

Rafe had washed her hair and soaped her body, stroked his big hands so gently over her stomach she'd almost cried, and made sure her every nook and cranny was thoroughly cleaned.

But would he let her do the same for him? Nope. He was steadfastly sticking to his "keeping his dick in his pants" rule. Figuratively, if not literally.

So every time she tried touching him in any way even remotely sexual, attempted to stroke his magnificently huge erection or cup his balls or even fondle his arse, he'd slapped her hands away, pinned her to the wall and kissed her neck, fondled her breasts. Fingered her pussy.

He'd driven her crazy with lust and wanting.

Thankfully he was also sticking to his nightly regime of going down on her until she screamed his name.

Her melancholy momentarily forgotten, her body shook with silent laughter.

He smiled against her hair. "That's better."

"What's better?"

"You've been so serious since we left Melville's Cross," he said. "Wanna tell me what's up?"

She leaned her forehead against his chest. "This doesn't feel right."

Pulling back a little so he could look at her, his brow arching upwards, he said, "It feels pretty nice to me."

A small smile tugged at one corner of her mouth. "I don't mean the hug. I like the hug. A lot."

"Good."

"I mean about you buying out my lease. I don't feel right about it. It's asking too much of you."

"You didn't ask. I offered."

"And that's another thing," she continued, instant irritation pulling her out of his embrace. "You barging headlong into my problems and fixing everything."

Instant *irrational* irritation.

Rafe cocked one brow at her but he didn't seem upset by her sudden outburst. More... amused. And that just annoyed her more. "You don't want me to fix your problems?"

"Yes. No." She threw her hands in the air. "I don't know. Maybe? I just... I hate relying on other people. And it's not that I don't appreciate everything you're doing. I do, really I do. But I only asked you to read an email. I never expected you to buy out my debts. I made this mess and I should be able to clean it up on my own. And I hate that I can't. I hate—" Angry tears burned behind her eyes, threatening to destroy what little composure she had left.

How did she explain this to him? How did she make him, Rafe, yet another successful overachiever understand what she was going through? That she'd always felt like she was two steps behind everyone else, that her best wasn't good enough, that despite the image she projected to the world at large she knew in her heart she was sorely lacking.

Inadequate.

"What?" Rafe prompted.

Dropping her chin to her chest, Jane felt her tears escape as she was forced to admit her shortcomings out loud.

"I'm the first Melville in a hundred years to fail at something." Then she flashed him a watery smile and gave him two thumbs up, attempted to put a brave face on her shame. "Go, me!"

The urge to punch Jane's father made Rafe grind his teeth. The pressure he'd put on both his children to perform to such unrealistic standards, to uphold the moralistic magnitude of the Melville name, was ridiculous.

He hated seeing the depth of Jane's doubt, hated hearing the hitch in her voice and the downtrodden finality that she was an unequivocal failure.

Cupping her face in his hands, he made her look at him. "You haven't failed, Jane. Not yet."

She glared up at him and he had to bite back a grin of approval. She had too much fire in her in wallow in self-pity for too long. "What would you call it then?"

"A set back. Nothing more."

She grabbed his wrists and pulled his hands away from her face, undoubtedly so he could witness the full force of her incredulity. "You call losing my life savings to an egotistical oxygen thief and landing myself in a world of debt that I can never repay, a 'set back'?"

"Yes. And it's not even that if you think about it."

Her mouth moved but no sound came out, and Rafe discovered he really enjoyed rendering his lover speechless, gaining the upper hand. She stalked a few paces away, spun on her heel and marched right back to him.

Drilling her finger into his chest, she found her voice and spluttered, "You are the most—"

Setting his grin free, Rafe stared down at Jane with unabashed amusement. "Handsome?" he offered. "Generous? Sexy? Amazing? Well endowed? Come on, Janie. One little adjective and we'll have a whole sentence."

"Arrogant, egotistical bastard!"

Rafe's smile widened. "There's my girl."

"What?" She spat the word at him.

Standing tall, he said, "I've been waiting for you to pick a fight with me since we left home. I thought you might last night at dinner but you backed off."

"We were in the middle of a restaurant. I wasn't going to fight with you in public."

"Why not? It wouldn't've been the first time."

"One time, Rafael," she snarled, poking him in the chest again. "That happened one time in my mother's café and I was eleven years old. And I fail to see what that has to do with this."

"It has nothing to do with it," he admitted. "Unless we're talking about your inability to back down from a fight. You've always fought for what you want, Jane. I've always admired that about you. And you may not have known what you wanted when you were a kid but you know what you want now." He grabbed her upper arms and held her tight. "Fight for it."

"But the money...." Her voice trailed off and her face tightened. Rafe knew that look. She was at war with herself, her logical brain fighting against her passionate heart. Jane had so much pride, and that coupled with her stubborn nature was what made her one of the most determined women he'd ever known.

What Sam Lyndon had done to her with his lies and ultimately his betrayal had put one hell of a dent in her pride, crushed her determination. Made her forget who she was. What she was.

She was fierce.

Fearless.

She just needed a gentle reminder, a nudge in the right direction.

"No one ever said this would be easy, baby," he cooed, stroking her hair, soothing her, "But no one said you had to do it alone either. And if you'd pull your head out of your arse and think about it for a moment, you'd see I'm right."

"My head isn't up my arse," she growled through gritted teeth.

"No? Because if you were thinking clearly you would have seen the solution the moment I offered to buy out your lease."

"Stop speaking in riddles or I'll flambé your arse."

Rafe spread his arms wide and grinned. "Two words, beautiful. Silent. Partner."

Before she could respond, a beautifully restored vintage Holden ute drove through the open gates and parked in front of the warehouse.

Rafe stood tall and his grin vanished as he switched into lawyer mode. He walked forwards to greet the man climbing out of the car. "Mr Bridges? I'm Rafael Bennett. We spoke on the phone yesterday."

"Ah, yes, good morning. My, you got here early, didn't you?"

Just by looking at him, Rafe couldn't quite tell if Mr Bridges was old or had simply led an eventful life.

His hair was grey with patches of silver and his skin, that which was visible, was tanned and leathery and covered in the blueish-green ink of old tattoos. His voice, however, seemed younger than the rest of him appeared to be.

"Good morning, Mr Bridges," Jane said, holding out her hand to shake the old man's. "Remember me?"

A brilliant smile lit the man's face and put a twinkle in his milky blue eyes. "Miss Melville! How could I forget you, or your maple pecan tart?" The old man leaned closer and whispered conspiratorially, "I don't suppose you brought another one with you?"

Jane smiled but it didn't reach her eyes. "No, I'm sorry. I didn't have time to bake anything for you. The decision to fly down was very last minute."

She glanced at Rafe and he moved to stand behind her, rested his hands on her shoulders. Let her know he was there for her.

Reassure her.

Mr Bridges patted her hand and offered her a kind smile, then unlocked the door and ushered them inside.

"Yes, yes. Your lawyer friend here told me all about your unpleasant situation over the phone. I wish I could help you out, sweetheart, I really do, but I can't afford to lose that much money, especially on a job that is already completed and not likely to sell to anyone else.

"A mobile patisserie is not all that common. Most of the trucks I fix up are for burgers, pizza and coffee." He put the kettle on to boil. "I did have a run of French crepe trucks a few years back, but they almost all went bust inside of a year. Would you like a cup of tea?"

Jane shook her head. "No, thank you. I appreciate your

concern and I understand your point of view completely. It's just a shitty situation all round, I guess."

Rafe cleared his throat. "About the lease, I'd—"

Mr Bridges waved him off. "It's too early to talk about money." He turned to Jane again. "How about you come and see your truck. That's why you're here, isn't it? To take her home to sunny Queensland?"

A spark of excitement lit up Jane's face, followed closely by apprehension. She looked at Rafe again, as though asking for his permission and his heart ached at her loss of confidence.

He hadn't really noticed it at home, where she was surrounded by family and familiarity. Here, now, in this unfamiliar situation it was obvious she was second guessing herself.

The woman who had aced every test they'd thrown at her at one of the toughest culinary schools in the world, was scared and unsure.

If I ever see Sam Lyndon again I will sell his body for dog meat.

And he could too.

Rafe knew people.

He took Jane's hand and smiled. "I think she'd like that very much. And as her business partner, so would I."

Eyes wide, Jane opened her mouth to speak, then shut it again and nodded. Her lips twitched up in one corner. "Yeah. That sounds like a plan."

Rafe followed Jane and Mr Bridges through to the main floor of the warehouse. The outfitter flicked a switch on the wall, and as the lights flickered on he saw row after row of food trucks, vans and trailers in various stages of transformation.

Sitting out front was a large cream coloured van with a big pink logo on the side.

Street Sweets Mobile Patisserie.

"There she is. A '65 Chevy Step-Van with interior and paint as per your instructions. Whaddaya think?"

"She's beautiful," she said softly, her hands pressed to her cheeks and her voice filled to the brim with awe. "Can I look inside?"

"Of course." Mr Bridges handed Jane a set of car keys. "She's all your now."

Jane unlocked the van and climbed inside. A few seconds later she made a loud *squeee* noise and the van started rocking as though she were jumping up and down. Which he realised she probably was. She did that when she was excited.

Rafe smiled and shook his head, then noticed the outfitter watching him curiously. "Should we discuss payment now?" he asked, shifting once more into work mode. "I'd like to pay out the lease today."

The old man's eyebrows shot up and his jaw fell slack. "The whole amount?"

"Yes. Do you take cheques, or would you prefer a money transfer?"

As the two men finalised the transaction in Mr Bridges' office, the old man said, "How long have you two known each other?"

"We grew up together."

He grunted. "And how long have you been in love with her?" Rafe looked up sharply from the paperwork he was reading and Mr Bridges laughed. "I'm old, not blind," he said. "The other one, the scumbag who ripped her off, he never looked at her the way you do. Cold fish, that one." He shook his head. "Sure, he put on a good act, but you can always tell what a man's truly feeling by looking at his eyes."

He swivelled in his office chair to face his computer. "She looks at you differently too, by the way." He stopped typing and glanced at Rafe again. "Is the baby yours or the scumbag's?" When Rafe made a choking noise, the other man quickly added, "Never mind. None of my business. Ignore the nosy old man."

After a beat of silence, the knot eased from Rafe's tongue. "It's mine," he said quietly. "Jane and me, well, it's complicated."

The old man grinned and threw him a pitying look. "Women usually are."

Chapter Thirteen

"**D**o you want to stop in Parkes for the night or push on through to Dubbo?"

Jane looked up from her notebook, startled by the sound of Rafe's voice.

They'd travelled for the better part of the day in companionable silence, listening to music and not talking about her little dummy-spit that morning.

She was thankful for that, and as they'd driven out of the warehouse and headed for the highway, Jane had made a decision: shut up and go with the flow.

Was she happy about Rafe spending all his money on her? No. But was she grateful?

More than he would ever know.

She still didn't understand why he was doing it, but maybe it was time she stopped looking this particular gift horse in the mouth and accepted events for what they were.

A new beginning.

A terrifying thought.

Rafe looked exhausted. He'd been driving for most of the day, only letting Jane drive when he absolutely needed a break. No way was she letting him drive for another two hours.

"Parkes," she said. "There are some nice motels on the far side of town. At least there used to be."

"How do you know that?"

"I came here years ago for the Elvis Festival."

Rafe grinned. "You? At an Elvis festival? Do tell."

"A friend of mine from the culinary college was a *huge* Elvis fan and dragged a bunch of us along with her. God it was crazy. Every man and his dog were dressed up like Elvis. And I mean that literally. There were dog Elvises."

Jane smiled as she remembered. "Everywhere we went, guys were dressed in sparkly jumpsuits and thick black wigs. In January. In Australia." She shook her head. "How they didn't all spontaneously combust or pass out from heatstroke is beyond me."

Rich and melodious, Rafe's laughter wrapped around her like a warm blanket. She'd always liked his laugh. No. She'd always *loved* his laugh.

And his smile.

Not that he smiled often. Rafe was more of a grinner than a smiler, and when he grinned he gave the impression he knew something others didn't. He always looked so smug. Jane used to find the trait incredibly irritating. Now she found it rather endearing. And when he aimed that grin at her... *wow*.

That grin melted her panties faster than a hot pan melted butter.

"Are you hungry?"

Jane checked her watch. Almost 5:30. "I could eat. From memory there's a lovely little Italian joint over... that way," she said, pointing to the right, then frowned. "I think. *Oooh*... or Chinese? I could seriously go some plum duck and deep fried ice cream right now. Or pizza! Or steak. Do you want steak?"

Rafe pulled up to a red light and glanced over at her, grinning. "Cravings?"

She repressed a whimper of need at that deadly grin and pressed her thighs together. "No more than usual."

And not just for food.

"How about we get a little of everything and share?" Rafe suggested, easing the van forwards again when the light turned green.

Nodding, Jane agreed. "Sounds like a plan."

Ninety minutes later they'd checked into a motel, freshened up and began devouring their smorgasbord of local fare.

Jane laughed at the look on Rafe's face as she ate her plum duck and deep fried ice cream at the same time. She wasn't sure if he was afraid, intrigued or disgusted.

"Don't knock it 'til you try it," she said, waving a forkful in front of his mouth, then almost fell off her chair in shock when he tried it. And liked it. *Damn it.* She was hoping she wouldn't have to share.

"Damn this is good," he said, digging into the spaghetti carbonara from the Italian place she'd remembered. "I don't usually eat carbs."

Trying not to drool while staring pointedly at his lean, muscular torso, sarcasm dripped from her tongue. "No, really? I would *never* have guessed that."

His mouth twisted with chagrin but his eyes still held their mirth as he returned her open appraisal. "What else did we get?"

Jane pointed to each dish, all crammed together on the tiny dining table situated between them. "Slow roasted pork belly with caramelised pears and sweet potato chips, classic pepperoni pizza—I mean, really, why mess with perfection? —and vegetarian san choy bow."

Trying the pork next, Rafe's eyes rolled back and he let out a moan she'd only ever heard him utter in bed, usually right before he climaxed. "Oh my God, this is heavenly. Please tell me you know how to cook this."

Jane snagged a wedge of pear on her fork and shoved it in her mouth, if only to stop herself from leaping on Rafe, kissing the fuck out of him and losing the bet.

The bet she was finding it harder and harder to care about winning the more alone time she spent with Rafe.

Be strong.

At least at home she had other people around her to act as a buffer to his charming ways, but in the van where it was just the two of them and every little touch, every sideways glance and secretive smile was amplified by their close quarters?

The struggle was very real.

And as she sat watching Rafe attempt to eat san choy bow, saw how every bite he took resulted in little dribbles of sauce trickling over his chin, she felt herself drawn to him even more. He looked like a total dork. And Jane had never wanted to lick someone so much in her life.

Standing abruptly, the need to put distance between them overtook her. "I think I'd like to go to bed now," she announced.

Rafe stared at her, his eyes narrowed and his head tilted slightly to one side. "Are you okay?"

"I'm just tired. It's been a long day."

Nodding, he wiped his mouth with the back of his hand then licked and sucked at the sauce that had stuck there, his lips and tongue doing those sexy things they did when he was going down on her. She swallowed hard.

If Rafe noticed her tongue trailing on the floor like a cartoon dog staring at an oversized rump roast, he had the good manners not to mention it. For once. Jane wasn't sure what the next level up from eye-banging was, but she was definitely doing it.

Managing to pull herself together long enough to escape to the bathroom, she showered quickly and brushed her teeth, then pulled on her pyjamas and slipped into bed.

Rafe met her gaze as she pulled the covers up to her chin, his expression unreadable, then he disappeared into the bathroom.

In an attempt to ignore the pitter-patter of running water as it cascaded over Rafe's delicious body, Jane stuffed her head under the pillow.

It didn't help.

She could picture it in her mind as clear as day even without the sound effects. Could see his head tilted back, the water splashing against his upturned face, running down the strong column of his neck and over his broad shoulders. Knew it would stream down his chest and straighten the curls covering his pecs then continue downwards to the thick thatch of hair surrounding his perfect cock.

Jane could well imagine Rafe's big hands soaping himself up, could see the look of concentration on his handsome face as he cleaned his body with the same precision he completed every other task in his life.

And it didn't take any great imagination to call forth a picture of Rafe's hand around his cock, of the slow, smooth glide of his fist as he pumped it up and down his ever hardening shaft.

Shifting so the pillow was under her again, Jane turned her face into it and screamed.

Stupid.   Horrible.   Traitorous.   Bloody.   Fucking. Hormones.

Rafe emerged from the bathroom in a cloud of steam.

Naked.

Because of course he was.

Like her, and despite everything that had happened between them in the last 24 hours, he was still trying to win Charlie's bet. He didn't know he was a lot closer to winning than he realised.

Jane wanted him. Desperately. She'd told him as much in words and in the heated looks she threw his way every time he flashed one of those damnable grins at her.

But what did Rafe want? A kiss? A stupid, meaningless kiss. He'd had his mouth all over her body every night for the last three nights, so what was one little kiss on the lips worth to him?

Nothing.

After checking the door was locked, he flicked off the light and climbed into bed, wrapped his arm around her waist and curled his large body around her smaller one.

"Good night," she murmured, trying to ignore the thick erection flexing against her back.

Firm lips pressed against her shoulder in a distinct upwards curve. "Good night, beautiful."

Thinking she'd managed to evade any more talk for the night, she closed her eyes and willed herself to sleep, but her overactive imagination—and the handsome lawyer behind her—were making it near impossible.

"Jane?"

"Yes?"

"You're fidgeting. Everything okay?"

"I can't sleep," she grumbled.

His voice was practically a purr. "Want me to go down on you?"

She tried in vain to stop her mouth from kicking up at the corners. "I always want that," she said, half turning in his arms. "Then I always want more."

Rafe nuzzled against her neck and snuck his hand under her chemise to cup her breast, stroked the pad of his thumb over her nipple. "You know what you have to do if you want more, Janie."

Jane bit her lip and focussed on the pleasure he was causing, on the intense yet delicious ache spreading outwards from her nipple and rushing through her body, ending in a pulse of sensation in her clit. She pressed her thighs together and whimpered.

Rafe misread the sound. "Would being my wife really be so bad?"

No.

Being his wife wouldn't be bad at all.

In fact, it would be beyond wonderful. She knew that because that's exactly how she'd always imagined being with Rafe—properly being with him—would be. Wonderful. Magical. Beautiful. Special.

It's how their first kiss had been, how their first time had been. But then....

He'd left.

And how did she know he wouldn't leave her again?

"Why are you here?" she whispered.

She heard the frown in his voice. "What do you mean?"

Jane closed her eyes and prayed for strength. Did she really want to do this? Now, after all this time?

Yes.

"I mean why are you here, with me, on this road trip? Why bail me out of trouble? Why help me at all?"

His heavy sigh fanned across her neck. "Why not?"

Rolling over to face him, she glared at him in the dark as though he could see her. "Can you not do that, please?"

"Do what?"

"That lawyer thing you do where you answer every question with another question."

The bed wobbled and shook and she knew he was silently laughing at her. She shoved against his shoulder and his laughter grew in volume.

"Stop it, Rafe. I'm serious. Geez, when did our roles reverse? I'm supposed to be the pain in the arse and you're supposed to be the serious one."

His arms tightened around her and he pulled her closer, close enough to squash her belly and breasts against his chest and abdomen. The thin fabric of her pyjamas did little to buffer the erotic zing of sensation she felt at the full body contact.

"Maybe it's time to try something new," he said, lightly trailing one hand down her back.

Squirming and wriggling against him, she fought against the tickling sensation he lit up along her spine. Fought against the urge to rub herself up and down his rock-hard cock. He had to feel how wet she was, even through her panties.

Concentrate. "Maybe it's time you answered my question."

Rafe leaned his forehead against hers. "Janie." He sighed again. "You really are so much smarter than that."

Bristling at his jibe, she snapped, "So you keep saying. But if I really was that smart, I would have figured out by now what you're obviously not telling me."

"Baby—"

"And don't call me baby or beautiful or any of the other

171

little nicknames you call me that you know turn my brain to mush." Her strident voice filled what little space was left between them. "Tell me why you're here."

His soft sigh brushed over her lips, a gentle caress. "I didn't bail you out, I invested in a mate's business. I'm on this road trip with you because there is nowhere else I'd rather be, and because I wanted time alone with you, to convince you to marry me."

"But why?" she whispered, tears gathering, filling her eyes and threatening to spill out of her.

"Because I'm hopelessly in love with you."

Tears slid down her cheeks and soaked her pillow. "No. It's not true. You can't be in love with me."

Silence met her ears for what felt like an eternity, then he said, "Why not?"

"Because I'm not—" She blinked away her tears, tried to clear them from her eyes, and tried again. Her voice shook, "Because you're a good man, and you deserve someone so much better than me."

He pushed her hair away from her face, kissed her forehead. "Janie, there is no one better for me than you. It's always been you. No one else makes sense."

Jane closed her eyes and held her breath, then let the words whisper past her lips, asking the one question she'd always been too scared to give voice to.

"Then why did you leave?"

Rafe rolled onto his back and stared at the ceiling. Of all the questions he'd hoped she'd never ask, why did it have to be that one, and why did it have to be now?

He scrubbed his hands over his face, then threw back the covers and sat on the edge of the bed.

"Rafe?"

The hurt in Jane's voice made his heart clench. Reaching back, he felt for her hand and gave it a reassuring squeeze. "I'm here, baby."

He felt her moving around, then her hand rested on his shoulder and he could feel her hesitance. "Then answer me. *Please*. It's been sixteen years. Surely you can tell me now?"

"I promised I wouldn't," he said, then laughed. The sound was not a pleasant one. "You know what? Fuck it. I am sick and tired of keeping a promise to a man who hasn't upheld his end of the bargain. He was supposed to keep you safe. He failed."

"What are you talking about? What man?"

Rafe turned to find Jane kneeling in the centre of the bed, glad it was too dark to see her face overly well. "Your father."

He heard her suck in her breath well enough though. "What?"

Striding to the other side of the room, Rafe flicked on the lights then grabbed his jeans and dragged them on. He needed pants to have this conversation.

Pants and distance.

He paced the room as he tried to decide the best way to go about telling Jane the truth. A truth he'd kept from her for so long.

"Do you remember the night of my twenty-first birthday, when you snuck into my room and climbed into bed with me?"

She shifted uneasily. "You mean the night I offered you my virginity and you said no?"

Rafe glowered, his lips pressed together in a firm line. "I

was studying to be a lawyer and you were underage. Did you honestly think I was going to say yes?"

"I was only three weeks shy of legal," she mumbled, avoiding his gaze, his ire. "It was supposed to be your birthday present."

"Where the law is concerned, near enough isn't good enough." Stopping by the bedside, he reached out and stroked her cheek. "Besides, you gave me a better present," he said. "When you told me you loved me."

Jane closed her eyes and leaned into his touch. The urge to drag her down to the bed and take her almost overwhelmed him. But that would be taking the easy way out. And she had a right to know.

He moved away again and grabbed a chair, sat in front of her, faced her head-on. He needed her to see him, to hear him. And understand.

"The following afternoon, I received a visit from your father. He threw a punch at my head and threatened to kill me if I ever touched you again."

That got her attention. "He hit you?" she said, eyes wide and mouth open.

"Please. I grew up dodging punches from Oliver and the twins. I know how to duck."

Snapping her mouth shut, she pinned him with her intense green stare. "But how did he even know we'd been together?"

Rafe dragged a hand down his face. "I can only assume someone saw you leave my room in the morning and jumped to the wrong conclusion. And that someone told Alec."

"What happened next?"

"What do you think happened?" he said, his mouth

twisting at the abhorrent memory. "He accused me of raping his daughter."

All the colour drained from Jane's face and she looked like she might throw up. "No. He wouldn't— He *couldn't* possibly believe that."

Of course she wanted to defend her father. She'd looked up to him her entire life.

Even if he didn't deserve it.

"Whether he believed it or not is irrelevant. I told him exactly what happened that night, told him we were in love." Rafe barked a laugh and shook his head. "I even asked his permission to marry you. But he didn't want to hear any of it. Alec was adamant, he wanted me charged with rape. Do you understand what that means?"

Slowly, she nodded. "It would have ended your career before it even began."

"Worse than that, baby," Rafe said. "It would have ended your life before it began."

"I don't understand," she said, but Rafe could tell from the downward tilt of her chin and the darting of her eyes, she understood plenty. She just didn't want to accept it.

"Something like that would not have stayed quiet, and once the media got wind of it—and the media always does—there would have been no stopping it."

Shaking her head, silent tears streamed down her cheeks. "Dad would never have gone through with it. He was bluffing."

"I wasn't willing to take that chance. Alec was too angry to see sense. As far as he was concerned, I'd hurt you and he was going to make me pay. And yeah, eventually he would've figured out he'd made a mistake, but by then the damage would've been done. Even if I'd gone to court and proven my innocence, you would have forever been the girl who was raped by the son of the Archibald Prize-winning artist Ulysses Bennett. Do you really think I would've let that happen to you? You meant *everything* to me. I had to protect you from that. In this day and age, when every little thing we do is recorded and filed and shared...."

He scrubbed his hands over his head. "It would have followed you for years, everywhere you went, every school application, every job interview. No, I couldn't let that happen. Not to you."

Rafe left the chair to sit beside Jane. Cupping her cheeks in his big hands, he rested his forehead against hers. "You were my everything." He sucked in a lungful of air, breathed in her sweet scent and let his love for her wash over him. "You *are* my everything. So when Uly offered an alternative solution, I grabbed it with both hands."

"The scholarships to study overseas," she said, realisation dawning in her lovely eyes. "That's why you took them? That's why you left me?"

"I had to protect you. Even if it meant losing you."

"Why didn't you tell me?"

"Alec made me promise I wouldn't. Still, I wrote you letters while I was away, but when I returned home it was obvious you'd never received them. I think he wanted you to hate me. Doubt me, at the very least."

She let out a shuddering breath then sniffed back her tears. "I think it worked," she whispered. She shook her head. "This is all my fault."

"What are you talking about?" Rafe said, smoothing Jane's hair away from her face. "How is any of this your fault?"

"I knew what I was doing when I snuck into your room that night," she said, her face stricken. "I knew the law, I knew I was underage, and I still went through with it. I threw myself at you! It's my fault you had to leave."

"Janie." Rafe pulled her into his embrace and wrapped her in his arms. She tried to free herself, but he held on tighter. "You didn't do anything wrong. Neither of us did. You were as much a virgin when you left my room as you were when you snuck in there in the first place.

"And even after all this time and everything that's happened between us, I wouldn't change a damn thing about that night. Because you told me you loved me, and that was the best present anyone has ever given me. Except maybe this one," he added, sliding his hand over her stomach. "I love you, Jane." A short burst of laughter escaped him as he smiled down at her and shook his head. "And you win."

"Win what?" she said, dashing the tears from her cheeks.

"Charlie's stupid bet. I'll stop asking you to marry me," he said, "if you'll just fucking kiss me."

A frown pulled at her brow as Jane stared at Rafe, unsure she'd heard him correctly. "What?"

"You heard me, beautiful. I surrender. You win. Kiss me."

Her hand shook as she reached up to touch her fingertips to his cheek. Why? Why was she shaking? Was she nervous... afraid...? But as soon as her skin glanced over his, as soon as that ever present zing lit along her veins, it fired every single one of her neurons, called them to action until they marched to the sound of only one drum.

Her heart.

It pounded in her chest, smashing out a tattoo of need and want and desire. Rafe had told her to fight for what she wanted, so she would.

Sliding both hands over his shoulders, she pushed with all her strength, shoved him down on the bed and straddled his hips. "You do realise that if I kiss you, that's it? We're fucking."

Rafe threw one of those grins at her and tucked his hands behind his head. *Smug bastard.* "I'm counting on it."

With her eyes puffy and rimmed in red, a snuffly nose and tears drying on her cheeks, Jane felt about as un-sexy as she could get. But the way Rafe looked at her, the way his deep blue eyes darkened and his eyelids shuttered, the way his grin softened at the edges until all the cockiness was gone and only adoration remained, blew away her self-conscious fears. Quieted her doubts.

Loosened her tongue and let her truth spill free.

"I love you," she whispered.

"I know."

Shaking with laughter, Jane let her happiness guide her. She leaned down and kissed Rafe's throat, then nibbled and sucked and licked a slow, torturous path to his mouth.

When she finally pressed her lips to his, a low moan escaped them both. But instead of deepening the kiss, she pulled away. Rafe chased her, nipping her chin when he missed her mouth and making her laugh again.

In a lightning fast move, he wrapped one arm around her back then used his weight to reverse their positions. "Come here, woman," he said, looming over her, and took her mouth.

It wasn't a gentle exploration either, or a seductive tease, but a full frontal attack. It was a kiss filled with the confidence and swagger of a man who didn't make promises he didn't intend to keep. A kiss that broke down every wall she'd ever built around her heart and forced it into the light.

She drowned in that kiss.

But she came alive in it too.

Clutching the back of Rafe's head, Jane held him to her and gave as good as she got. Tongues tangled, teeth clashed and bodies writhed. Rafe sat back and yanked Jane's chemise over her head, then dragged her panties off too.

His zipper was down when he fell on top of her again, his thick erection nestled in the open V of his jeans. Jane hooked her toes in the waistband and pushed the well-worn denim over his magnificent arse and down his long legs.

Slipping his hand between them, he said, "Are you wet for me, baby?"

When she felt his finger glide along her wet slit then thrust inside, felt the rasp of his thumb on her clit, Jane could do little more than whimper and nod, but somehow she found the strength to speak. "Are you hard for me, lawman?"

Rafe's smile was fast and broad, and as his mouth found hers with unerring precision, so too did his cock glide smoothly inside her, filling her up until he bottomed out.

"Oh God!" she cried. "Even sex is better pregnant."

Rafe buried his face in the crook of her neck, his breathing laboured with masculine grunts. "You're so tight. *Jesus*. Am I hurting you?"

Jane arched her back and thrust her small, sensitive breasts against his muscled torso, abraded her nipples against his chest hair. *So good.*

"If this is pain, you can hurt me anytime you like."

A deep, rumbling chuckle vibrated through Rafe and into her, then he was kissing her again. Slower this time, deeper.

His lips plucked at hers in a teasing rhythm, made her chase him, want him, then he slid his tongue inside her mouth and licked along the length of hers, twisted and tangled and tasted.

How long they stayed locked together like that, Jane didn't know, but a wealth of feeling flooded through her the longer their lips were locked.

It was overwhelming, intimidating, and she felt a sudden need to pull the plug on the pit in her soul and let all the bad stuff drain away.

She wanted to move forward with Rafe with a clear conscience and a clean soul.

Locking her feet behind Rafe's arse, Jane wrapped her arms around his neck, gripped his head and held on. She wanted him close for what would come next. Needed him to hold her, see her. Forgive her.

She tore her mouth from his. "I love you, Rafael," she said. "And I'm sorry. I'm so sorry."

Rafe slowed his movements to a steady rocking motion and lifted himself onto his arms. His face hovered just above hers, his voice fanned her cheek. "You've done nothing to be sorry for."

"But I have," she whispered, staring into the devastating dark of his eyes. "You were right. I always ran out on you. Even after our first time." When he'd returned and she'd given him everything. "I left you more than you ever left me."

She shook her head, ashamed of the way she'd behaved. "At first I was being petty. I was young and stupid and wanted to pay you back for leaving me, but as time wore on and we got older, I left because—" She sucked in a shuddering breath, tried to force the words past the lump in her throat without crying. "Because I—"

"Was scared," Rafe finished.

Eyes wide, Jane searched Rafe's face. "How did you...?"

"Because I was scared too," he said, pulling out of her.

She was about to protest when he rolled her on her side, slid deep inside her pussy and spooned her. Her eyes rolled back and her mouth fell open on a moan as his cock hit her G-spot, again and again.

"Sixteen years," he growled, pumping his hips. "We've circled each other for sixteen fucking years and never got our timing right. And it was unfair of me to put all of that on you when I'm just as much to blame."

"No."

"Yes. I wanted you so much. Loved you so much. But I did nothing about it. Because what if...?"

Jane reached back and grabbed his hand. "What if we didn't work? What if after all that time, reality didn't live up to the fantasy? What then?"

"Exactly," he said. "But do you wanna know something?"

"What?"

His lips brushed the shell of her ear. "The reality of being with you far surpasses any fantasy my boring brain could ever concoct." He thrust faster, gripped her hip tighter. "Jane, you are the only woman I have ever truly wanted, and now I have you, I am never letting you go." Rafe gripped her chin and turned her head then smashed his mouth against hers.

"Rafe!" Jane tore herself away as her orgasm hit without mercy and spiralled out of control. She welcomed it, opened herself up to the sensation of total abandon and utter wantonness.

Rafe hooked his arm under her leg and lifted it higher, sank in deeper, then ploughed into her with such force the bed banged against the wall with every thrust of his hips. His grip on her body tightened to the point of pain but Jane didn't care.

They were together.

They were in this together.

As they always should have been.

Rafe's breathing grew as erratic as the thrusting of his hips until finally he slammed home once, twice, three times, then collapsed on the bed behind her.

Jane was little more than a quivering mess, a boneless puddle of blissed out, panting woman as Rafe tucked her into his side. He wrapped his arm around her and dropped a kiss on her forehead. "I won't ever leave you again, Janie. I promise."

She promised too. She was his, forever.

And he was hers.

Always.

"Rafe?"

"Uh-huh?"

"Did you really write me letters?"

He kissed the side of her face and she felt his smile linger against her temple. "Dozens of them."

Chapter Fourteen

The rest of the trip passed uneventfully enough, if Jane didn't count the blowjobs she'd given Rafe while he was driving, or the sex-a-thon in their motel room when they'd stopped for the night, or how she'd woken him up before hitting the road that morning: with her hair pulled up in ponytails and her tits bouncing in front of his face as she rode his cock like the prize bull at a rodeo. Until he'd toppled her over, held her down and driven into her like a man possessed.

Or like a man who'd thrown the fight because he was just as eager to claim the reward as she was.

Yeah, Jane was pretty sure Rafe had let her win that stupid bet. Not that he wouldn't have won it if he'd just waited another day.

She'd been on the verge of giving in, especially after her mini-meltdown in Melbourne and Rafe's subsequent rescue, not just of her business but of her sanity.

Silent partner.

She could have kissed him when he'd said those words.

Rafe knew her too well. He knew she'd never accept

anyone simply giving her money, knew her stupid pride would never allow her to accept charity of that magnitude. But a business partner? That was something her brain could wrap itself around. Guilt free.

And unlike her previous business partner, she knew she could trust Rafe not to screw her over.

That one gesture had helped her make the decision to go with the flow.

And that had turned out pretty well too.

They'd shared so much that first night on the road, less on the second as their libidos caught up with them, but Jane felt as though a weight had finally been lifted off her chest.

She could breathe again. Live again. The fear and the anger she'd clung to for sixteen years, that had filled that swirling pit of despair in her soul, was gone.

Drained.

Empty... except maybe for a few dregs.

But she'd tell Rafe about those too....

Later.

Right now she was just happy to be home. And that in itself was a miracle considering a big part of marrying Sam had been to get the hell outta Dodge.

It has been an eventful week.

But as she reached across the seat and rested her hand on Rafe's thigh, she realised that for the first time in ever, she felt... *content.*

Curling his fingers around hers, he said, "Do you want me to come with you when you speak with your father?"

"Yes." She nodded. "Please."

"Whatever you need, beautiful," he said, then lifted her hand and kissed her knuckles.

While Jane had looked forward to ending the road trip and relished the fact they'd no longer be stuck in the van all day, she was not looking forward to the coming confrontation with her father.

She still had trouble wrapping her head around what Rafe had told her, and it wasn't that she didn't believe him.

Jane simply didn't *want* to believe him.

She didn't want to think her father, a man she'd always considered a paragon of truth and a testament to what hard work and dedication could bring you in life, could be capable of such hateful actions.

She wanted to see her mum. Had to talk to her first. Because if anyone could shed a little extra light on the situation, it was her.

Were Rafe's recollections tainted by time and anger? Or was his truth the whole truth? Had her father really orchestrated the breaking of her heart under the guise of keeping her safe? From Rafe?

A man her father had once described as the human equivalent of a beige Volvo.

Not just boring. *Safe* and boring.

"Can you park outside the café, please? I need to see mum. And I want to show her the van. I've been telling her about the bloody thing for so long that if—"

Her words choked off as Rafe rounded the corner onto Main Street.

A police vehicle was parked in front of her mother's café, and Sergeant Scott Turner was leaning against the side of the Land Cruiser, sipping from a coffee mug and nodding along to whatever her mother was telling him. He straightened at the sight of them pulling up behind his cruiser.

Jane leapt from the van the moment Rafe put it in park and raced to her mother's side. "Mum! What's wrong? What's happened?"

But from the corner of her eye she could see exactly

what had happened. Turning to stare at the patisserie, Jane took in the scene before her. Four giant letters, scrawled in red spray paint stretched to cover the entire shopfront.

SLUT

A quick glance to the left and right of the café revealed none of their neighbours had received such colourful language splashed across their shop windows, meaning Straight to the Hips had been targeted.

And Jane doubted very much anyone had to balls to call Mary Melville a slut.

No. This had happened because of her.

Her voice felt like sandpaper in her throat as she stared at the graffiti. "Where's dad?"

Her mother's voice sounded even more raw than her own and Jane put her arm around her shoulders. "In Sydney." At Jane's frown, Mary added, "He's with your brother. He won't be home for a few days."

Jane turned to Scott. "Do you have any idea who might have done this?"

The sergeant's mouth tightened. "No. I don't. We have had an uptick in graffiti around town though, so it's possible it's related to that."

"But you don't think so," Rafe said. It wasn't a question.

"Mary was telling me you had an incident in the store the other day, with Patricia Leighton."

"Oh, Scott, really," Mary said, rolling her eyes. "You can't possibly think that stuck-up cow would do something like this. She might break a nail."

Scott handed her the coffee mug. "That's what I love about you, Mary, you never mince words."

"It saves time," Mary and Jane said together, and shared a short-lived but affectionate laugh.

"Leave it with me," Scott said. "It's probably just bored

kids but it doesn't hurt to ask around." Then he climbed back in his cruiser and drove away.

"Are you all right, Mary?" Rafe asked. "Have you called Alec?"

Mary swiped a stray tear from her cheek and looked up at Rafe. "I'm fine, and yes, I called him. He was going to come back today but I told him not to. There's nothing he can do here. And Richard needs him more than I do right now."

"Why?"

"Laura won't let him see the kids," she explained.

"Maybe I should give him a call," Rafe said, shocking the hell out of Jane.

After Richard had cheated on and then divorced their sister, the Bennett brothers had essentially made it their life's mission to make Richard's life hell at every given opportunity.

Mary cocked one brow and shot Rafe a severe look. "Why?"

"Because I'm in love with your daughter and I fully intend to marry her," he said. "And what sort of brother-in-law would I be if I didn't offer my services. I do specialise in family law, after all."

Jane's eyes widened and her cheeks felt hot. "Rafe!"

Mary snickered. "Sounds like you two had an eventful trip. Come inside and tell me about it."

Jane followed her mother but Rafe pulled out his phone. "I'll be there in a tick."

Once inside, Jane surveyed the damage again. It didn't look as bad from inside the shop, still, it was bad enough that Jane reconsidered asking her mum about Rafe and her dad. Especially since it was almost lunchtime and there wasn't a single customer within cooee of the place.

"What's on your mind, baby?"

Jane shook her head. "It can wait. You have more important things to think about."

"Not really," Mary said, as she pulled down three mugs and started making coffee. "Although, I suppose I could start planning your wedding. Have you set a date?"

Scowling at her mother's impish grin, she said, "Don't encourage him."

"Don't encourage whom?" Rafe said, shutting the door behind him. "Dad and the others are coming down to help clean off the graffiti. Uly says he has something that will take off the paint without damaging the glass." Mary nodded her thanks then handed Rafe a coffee. "Thanks."

When she handed one to Jane, Jane looked at Rafe who was scowling at Mary.

"Is that decaf?" he growled.

"Now why on Earth would I serve my own daughter a big ol' cup of steaming disappointment."

"She's not supposed to be drinking caffeine," he grumbled.

"Rubbish. One cup a day won't hurt," Mary said, then cocked a brow at his continuing glare. "You do recall that I'm married to a doctor, yes?"

"How about this," Jane said, keeping her tone reasonable. "You let me drink one cup of *normal* coffee a day, and I won't cut your balls off in your sleep. Okay?"

That night, as they sat in bed, Jane rubbed at a smudge of red paint on her hand. "I feel like Lady Macbeth," she joked. "Out, damn spot."

Rafe smiled as he watched her. His family had spent

the afternoon cleaning the graffiti off the patisserie's shopfront while he and Jane had spoken with Mary, who had confirmed his version of events from sixteen years ago.

He'd hated the look of devastation that had dulled Jane's lovely eyes at the news. Hated her father even more for it. That look still lingered in her gaze, even now, hours later, and Rafe knew he couldn't let it fester.

"Do you want to talk about it?"

"About Macbeth?"

No. The other betrayer. "About your father."

She fidgeted by his side and finally abandoned the smudge of paint on her hand as a lost cause. Sighing quietly, she said, "Why didn't he just ask me about it? Why hide it from me?"

"Because he wanted to protect you. Like your mum said."

Mary hadn't had a lot to say about it, but she did mention Jane's age at the time being their main reason for interfering. "She was so young, Rafael."

She'd also confirmed Jane's theory that her father was bluffing about taking Rafe to court, that he'd banked on Rafe wanting to do the right thing by Jane and would do just about anything to protect her.

Even abandon her.

His blood still boiled over that little revelation.

"That's bullshit. More likely he didn't trust me to tell him the truth," Jane said, pulling him back to their current conversation. "No matter what I do, it's never enough for him. I'm just his vacuous twit of a daughter. No filter and no common sense."

Rafe scowled at the hurt, the vehemence in her voice. "You know that's not true."

"What I know is my father deliberately separated me

from the man I loved because he thought I was too naïve to know my own mind. My own heart. And...."

"And?"

"I've done some really dumb things in my life, Rafe. And all just to avoid ever going through that sort of heartache again. Because the day you left, was the worst day of my life."

She hung her head. "I need to tell you something." She sniffed. "You're not going to like it and you're probably going to rethink being with me after you hear it, but I have to tell you. I don't want there to be any more secrets between us," she said. "It's about Sam."

Steeling himself for whatever bomb Jane was about to drop, Rafe sat up a little straighter.

Resisting the urge to put his arms around her, he said, "Hit me with it."

"Him and me, our relationship, our marriage." She took a deep breath. "It was all a lie."

Rafe's eyes narrowed and his hands curled into fists beneath the blanket. "Explain."

Jane flinched at his tone, but Rafe couldn't help it. The mere mention of her ex-fiancé made his temper swell to the point of exploding.

"It was a marriage of convenience," she said. "I had the ideas and the money to back them, and Sam had the contacts in Melbourne and the know-how to make things happen. He was supposed to be my business partner. He was supposed to be my friend. He—"

"He was a conman, Janie," Rafe said, his anger dissolving to nothing at the sound of her distress. He tugged her into his arms and held her against his chest, stroked her hair.

"Yeah, and he saw me coming a mile away," she grumbled. "It was so stupid! I was so stupid. I lost everything and reinforced my father's opinion of me in one fell swoop."

Rafe had come across enough liars and thieves in his time to know even the smartest people got conned, and despite Jane's belief to the contrary, he had zero intentions of rethinking their relationship.

It would take a lot more than that to scare him off.

But his curiosity did get the better of him. "Who's idea was it to get married?"

"Mine. On the off chance I needed more capital, banks are still more willing to lend money to someone with a penis than without."

That did make sense. It also explained why she'd given Sam access to her accounts. But he still cocked one brow and stared down at her upturned face. "You're sure it was your idea?"

Jane's brow furrowed and her eyebrows pinched together. "Yes," she said, dragging the word out. She didn't sound very sure. "Why?"

"Sam is a con artist, baby. It is literally his job to make other people think his bad decisions are their brilliant ideas then thank him for his time." And then another thought struck him. Only, he wasn't sure he wanted to know the answer to his next question. "And the whole swinger thing? His idea, or yours?"

Her mouth twisted with disgust. *Interesting.* "His. Definitely his. And while we're on the subject...."

"Yes?" It was his turn to stretch out the word.

Pink stained her cheeks and she ducked his gaze. "I never actually participated. In the swinging."

"Umm... what?" Rafe definitely needed clarification for that one.

"I never swung, okay? Swang? Swinged? Whatever. I never had sex with anyone at those stupid parties."

He choked back his laughter. "You went to sex parties, but never actually had sex?"

Jane scowled up at him as his body shook with his amusement. "Shut up," she said, elbowing him in the ribs. "Have you seen the people who go to those things? They are creepy. With a capital *ugh*." She shuddered. "I usually ended up in the kitchen making sandwiches or sitting in the corner nursing a beer and talking to the cat."

"You should have called me," Rafe said, stroking her hair away from her face. "I would have rescued you."

"Rescuing me seems to have become your full-time job," she grumbled.

"I can think of worse things to occupy my time," he said, sliding down in the bed so his mouth was level with her perfect breasts. Her blissfully naked, perfect breasts. He laved her nipple with the broadside of his tongue and revelled in the feel of the sexy pink tip hardening under his touch. Matched her wanton moan with one of his own.

"Rafe." Her hands slid over his scalp and forced him closer. "More."

"How much more, beautiful?"

"All of it," she sighed. "All of you."

"As you wish."

Rafe made short work of getting Jane under him, of sucking and biting her nipples until they were dark pink and as hard as rubies.

He loved the way she arched her back, as though she were trying to shove her breast deeper in his mouth. When he tried to tease her and pull away, she grabbed his head in both hands, her fingernails scoring his skull as she dragged him back down.

Fierce little woman.

Methodically, he worked his way down her body and back again, kissing and licking, touching, feeling, learning. Her body was changing, growing more sensitive every day, and he loved discovering new ways to turn her on, new ways to make her sigh or cry out or moan in pleasure.

By the time he slid his hard cock deep inside her warm, wet pussy, she was a writhing bundle of sexually taut nerves, begging him for release. And he was more than happy to oblige.

Holding his weight off her, Rafe rocked his hips, rolled them against her lithe little body and the new softness he felt there. She'd started gaining weight with the pregnancy, had started rounding out in several places. He liked it.

Not that he hadn't liked her body before—he loved her petite little figure, even if it made him feel like a giant when he stood before her, naked.

But this new softness, these extra curves, he didn't how to describe it or why, but they did things to him. Made him want her even more than usual. Made that sense of pride he felt every time he stroked his hand over her swollen belly want to stand up and crow, victorious. "I did this!"

A broad grin stretched across his face at the thought and he knew Jane would thump him if he ever said something so Neanderthalish out loud.

"What are you grinning at?" she said between panted breaths.

"Just enjoying the feel of my big dick inside your insanely tight cunt." She squeezed her body around his shaft and Rafe's eyes rolled back in his head.

"How do you do that?"

"Do what, baby?"

"Make a word as crude as cunt sound sexy as hell."

His grin grew. "It helps that everyone thinks I'm too boring to even know what the word means," he said, then enjoyed the way her muscles clenched around his cock when she laughed.

"Oh God, Rafe. I'm going—to—" Jane cried out as her release hit, her body clamping so tightly around Rafe's cock he couldn't have held back his own orgasm if he'd tried. He followed on her heels, yelling her name as did. He didn't even care that his whole family probably—definitely—heard them.

We need our own place.

Gathering her in his arms, he said, "Move in with me."

Jane rested her chin on his chest. "Move in here?"

"For now," he said. "But I was thinking, there are a few places up for sale on the other side of town, and we're going to need our own place eventually."

"*Our* place?"

He tightened his arms around her. "Yes, our," he repeated. "Whether you marry me or not, Janie, I'm never letting you go again."

Chapter Fifteen

The next morning passed in a blur in what felt like an endless merry-go-round of trips between her parent's house and The Forge, as Jane and Abby transferred all of Jane's belongings to her new home, giggling like twelve year olds the entire time.

Rafe had offered to help but Jane had declined. One, because she wanted to spend some girl time with her BFF, and two, because Rafe had enough to do, first making space for her in his room, then finishing up at his office, getting ready to open for business on Monday morning.

After a celebratory lunch of fish and chips—because moving in with the man of your dreams should always be celebrated—Jane and Abby took over the kitchen.

"This feels familiar," Abby said, sitting at the table with her sketchpad and charcoal in hand while Jane sifted flour into the cake mixture she was making. "I've missed this."

It'd been several months since they done anything like this. Probably closer to a year. The sifter's metallic *shushing* ceased as Jane's hands stilled over the bowl. "I've been a really crappy friend this year, haven't I?"

The truth of it hit her like a bullet train and her knees wobbled, threatening to give out beneath her. Abby leapt to her feet and grabbed Jane around the waist, eased her into a chair. The sifter bounced where it landed on the table in a tiny cloud of flour.

"You've had a lot on your plate this year," Abby said. "That doesn't make you a crappy friend."

But Jane knew the truth.

She'd been more demanding, more temperamental, and less attentive to things, to people who deserved better. "I'm sorry, Abby," she said. "For all the stress I caused you over Richard and Wolf and the engagement party and the wedding and everything, and for being bossy and interfering and I honestly don't know why you put up with me—"

"Jane."

"Shutting up," she said.

Abby smiled at her, laughed, then pulled her into a hug, enveloped her in warmth and the scent of rose scented soap. "I put with you because I love you. And I love you because you may come across as a loony-toon, but anyone who truly knows you, knows you'd do anything for the people you love. And without you and your bossy interference, I wouldn't have ended up with Wolf. So thanks for that."

Jane laughed and wiped her tears away. *Stupid hormones making her cry again.* "I love you, Abbs."

Her friend shrugged. "So you should. I'm awesome."

Jane laughed again, louder, harder, and just like that, she knew everything was going to be okay.

Jane rummaged through the box marked "misc. bed."

searching for the spare phone charger she was sure she'd packed that morning. What she found instead was infinitely more important.

Small and unassuming, the gift she'd wrapped in plain blue paper, stared up at her.

Not quite taunting her, but also not *not* taunting her.

She'd searched for it for months, then angrily shoved in it in a drawer and promptly forgot about it after the Great Phone Call Sidestep.

But as Rafe moved around the room behind her, she lifted the gift out of the cardboard box, stared at it a moment longer, then thrust it towards him before she changed her mind and hid it again. "Here."

"What's this?" He smiled. "A house-warming present?" His smile fell. "I didn't get you anything."

She laughed at his expression, then shook her head. "No. Before you started ducking my phone calls, I went shopping for an apology gift." He raised one brow and turned the gift over in his hands. "To say sorry about our fight after the picnic," she clarified, then folded her arms over her chest and pursed her lips. "I don't actually *enjoy* fighting with you, you know?"

Lips twitching into a grin, his gaze flicked towards hers. "All evidence to the contrary."

"Fine," she said, holding her hand out. "Give it back."

Rafe held his arm above his head, well and truly placing the gift out of Jane's reach. "Nope. It's mine now. And I'm gunna open it."

Nervous tension wound itself tight around Jane's gut and she turned back to her boxes of junk, closed her eyes, breathed through it... until she heard the wrapping paper rip and the urge to vomit had her sitting on the edge of the bed and thrusting her head between her knees.

"Seven Little Australians," he said with something akin to wonder in his voice, then crouched down in front of her.

Jane lifted her head just enough to meet his gaze. "You always said it was your favourite book when you were little."

Because he was Ulysses Bennett's seventh child.

He smiled. "Yes, I did." Then he cupped her cheek and kissed her, long and deep. "Only you would remember something like that." He shook his head, chuckled. "Sometimes I think you know me too well."

She snorted. "Oh, I don't know. I think that ex-assistant of yours prides herself on knowing you better than anyone."

Rafe kissed her again then leaned his forehead against hers. "She doesn't know about the book."

Jane smiled, happy. Happy she'd made him happy. "You really like it? I mean, it's not a first edition or anything like that."

"It's perfect," he said, then slid the small hardcover edition onto the bedside table. "I love it." He shifted her box of crap to the side, slowly eased her onto her back, then crawled over the top of her. "And I love you."

Jane sighed and lolled her head to one side, granting Rafe access to her neck. His lips were hot against her skin as he trailed kisses from her jawline to her collarbone, and she sucked in a gasp when his tongue dipped into the hollow at the base of her throat.

Slowly, he licked a path up her neck and over her chin, driving her crazy with the feather-light touch that ended with his lips plastered to hers, searing her flesh with his passionate kiss.

Boring bastard, my arse.

"Rafe," she murmured against his mouth. "I love you."

His hand slid under her T-shirt and stroked the sensitive skin below her breast. "Say it again." Though whispered, the words were harsh, raw, and this time when his lips met hers, his teeth joined in, nipping at her, biting. Gently, he grazed his teeth over her cheek and along her jaw then down, down until he was sucking on the flesh at the base of her throat, marking her for all to see.

She was his.

"I love you," Jane repeated, a smile a mile wide decorating her face as his hand slid higher and cupped her breast. Devious fingers weaselled their way under her bra, finding more skin to sweetly torture. Plucking at her nipple until she arched into him and moaned. "I should buy you books more often."

She felt his smile press into the crook of her neck. "You don't need to bribe me to make love to you, Janie."

Faking a spluttering cough and pressing her hand to his chest to hold him at bay, she said, "You think that was a bribe?"

Smiling broadly, Rafe replied, "I think... I should shut up before I stick my foot even further in my mouth."

When Jane laughed he kissed her again and she melted against him. His teeth, his tongue, his whispering breath, all worked together to seduce and enchant her.

But then he shifted his weight off her and rolled to her side, stroked her forehead and brushed a lock of hair away from her face.

The look in his dark blue eyes gave her chills. The good kind, edged with that excited feeling that made her tingle all over and crave more of them. And that look... she knew what was coming. Hell, he'd managed to go for—she counted in her mind—two whole days without bringing it up again.

Jane held her breath and waited.

"Will you marry me?"

Bingo!

"Nuh-uh. You lost the bet. You're not allowed to ask me that anymore."

"I also said I wouldn't fuck you until you agreed to marry me, and correct me if I'm wrong but we've been having some pretty phenomenal sex."

She didn't correct him.

His smile grew predatory. "In fact, I think we should have some more."

Grinning like a lunatic, Jane slid her hands between them, felt for the button on his jeans. "Rafe...."

Rafe did the same and had her pants halfway down her arse before someone banged on their bedroom door and rattled the handle, trying to get in.

"Rafe! Jane! Now!" Oliver's voice boomed through the door, his urgency tinged with anger.

Without a word, Rafe leapt off the bed and refastened his jeans, yanked the door open and followed the sounds of chaos echoing through the house.

Jane quickly followed and found herself standing on the front veranda, staring in horror at a spot by the roadside.

Her old Jeep was engulfed in bright orange flames.

"Janie, get back inside," Rafe yelled, pushing her towards the front door before grabbing the fire extinguisher Oliver was shoving at him and bolting down the stairs, running towards the burning car.

Jane didn't move.

She couldn't.

Her feet were frozen to the spot as she stared, wide-eyed, at the scene unfolding before her.

Plumes of thick black smoke billowed from the tops of the raging flames. Faded yellow paint curled away from the metal as the fire chased it, crackling and popping, across the rusted surface of the car.

Rafe, Oliver, Abby and Wolf attacked the flames from all sides with fire extinguishers and the garden hose, wetting it down, slowly bringing the flames under control.

Until the windscreen cracked and something boomed and the window exploded outwards in a ball of fire, knocking Rafe down and showering him in glass.

"Rafe!"

Jane tried to run to him but a strong arm banded around her middle and held her back.

"Don't." Ulysses barked the order. "He's all right."

She struggled against the old man's grip even as she watched Rafe get to his feet and shake his head, as though dazed. "Let me go, Uly."

"He has enough to worry about without you going down there too," he hissed in her ear, and she heard the worry in his craggy voice. "You think I don't want to race down there and help them? Those are my children."

His children.

His children who were in danger because of her. Jane ceased fighting and he loosened his grip on her.

"We would only be in their way, love. They've trained for this. Let them work."

Rafe looked up at her then and nodded, a brief tilt of his head to let her know he was okay before grabbing another fire extinguisher and pulling the pin. Jane clutched at her chest, at the place where her heart thudded so hard she wasn't sure it was good for her.

He's all right.

Squaring her shoulders and straightening her spine, she turned towards the front door. "I'm going to make some tea," she announced, clenching her jaw to hold back the tears she felt threatening to fall. "And sandwiches. Fire-fighting calls for sandwiches."

A kind smile lifted Uly's lips. "That's a fine idea." And as she pulled open the screen door, she heard the sound she knew they'd all been waiting for, and her relief let her tears escape.

Sirens.

Rafe set the fire extinguisher down by his feet then used his T-shirt to wipe the sweat from his brow. "I'm out," he called to his siblings.

"Me too," Ollie said, pulling back from the fire.

Abby was on to her third extinguisher, a steely look of determination in her dark brown eyes as she bravely attacked the flames. But Wolf had backed away from the car and begun hosing down the rose bushes on the other side of the stone wall bordering his sister's garden.

Being so close to the fire, they'd started smouldering, and his future brother-in-law had obviously decided a rescue attempt was in order, especially now the fire brigade was barrelling up Bennett's Road, sirens blaring and lights flashing.

Thirty seconds later, two Land Cruisers pulled to a halt in front of The Forge. The first was Scott's police cruiser, the second was the local Rural Fire Service vehicle. Rafe stepped back, pulling Abby with him, giving the firies room to move and do their job.

His sister let out a growl of frustration and dropped the empty fire extinguisher on the ground at her feet.

Ollie helped drag her back to the veranda, where she collapsed into Wolf's arms and watched in defeat at the sight of the fire taking hold again. Rafe chucked her under her chin and offered her a small smile. His baby sister felt everything so deeply.

Scott made his way over to where they sat on the stairs. He wasn't in uniform though, dressed instead in blue jeans, leather boots and a dress shirt.

Doctor Chen walked by his side with a first aid kit in her hand, her usual doctor's garb replaced with a flowing floral dress that accentuated her athletic figure. Her hair was down too, and her lips now held a distinct shade of red she hadn't been wearing when he'd seen her in the clinic.

And Rafe wasn't the only one to notice.

"I hope our little emergency didn't interrupt anything," Ollie said, a hint of... *something* souring his tone. Jealousy, perhaps? But that didn't seem right.

"Stop pouting, pretty boy," Scott said. "You had your chance."

Marie shot a look at the police Sergeant, one brow raised. "You want a second date?" she said, leaving no room for doubt she'd dump his arse here and now if he said the wrong thing.

"Ah... yeah."

"Then zip it." Then she turned to Rafe and narrowed her gaze as she looked him over. "You have glass stuck in your face."

"Shit. That'll be from the exploding window." Gingerly, he touched his cheek where it hurt the most and felt the tiny shard of glass. "Can you get it out before Jane sees it? She's freaking out enough as it is."

Snapping on a pair of latex gloves, the doc went to work. Rafe sat as still as possible as she tweezed out the glass and cleaned the wound, which meant grinding his teeth together so tightly he thought his molars would crack.

"You don't need stitches," she said. "Steri-strips will do fine. Just keep the wound clean and re-apply the strips if needed."

"Thanks, Doc."

"Anyone else?" she asked, pulling off her gloves and reaching for a fresh pair. But his siblings all declined the offer, and by the time Marie packed up the first aid kit, Jane's Jeep was a smouldering heap of scrap metal, broken glass and melted plastic.

But at least the fire was out.

The head of the local brigade strode with purpose towards their little gathering on the veranda.

James Turner had been the co-ordinator of the RFS for as long as Rafe could remember. All the Bennett's had trained under him at Ulysses' insistence, and Oliver still volunteered when they needed an extra pair of hands during bushfire season.

He was also the good police Sergeant's father.

"Evening all," he said, lifting his hand in greeting.

The older man opened his mouth to say more but the screen door swung open and banged against the wall of the house. Ulysses appeared, carrying a tray of mugs and a large thermos. "Evening, James."

"Uly."

Then Jane brought out a tray filled with sandwiches and the tiny honey cakes she'd baked that afternoon and set them down, and suddenly four more firefighters appeared out of the darkness.

"Amazing how fast they pack up when there's free food to be had," James said, winking at Jane, then raised his voice. "Of course if it's not packed away correctly, the whole team while be running suicide sprints for a week."

A collective groan sounded as the four disappeared

again. "Save us some," one of them threw over their shoulder.

"What's the damage, James?" Rafe said.

The fireman looked at Jane. "Did you store a jerry can in your car?"

She shook her head and frowned. "No."

James sighed and rubbed the back of his neck. "Then I'm gunna go with arson."

Anchoring his hands on his hips, Scott hung his head and swore. "Shit."

"I'll have to do an official investigation, mind you, to be absolutely certain," James continued, "But I saw what looks to be the remains of a jerry in the front seat."

"That'll be what blew the windscreen out," Abby said. "When the pressure in the can blew."

The old fiery grunted. "Whomever it was probably thought the whole car would explode. Thank Christ for the dumb ones. That said, it could have been a lot worse. Well done, you lot, for keeping it under control until we got here. The last thing any of us needs at this time of year is a fire getting away from us."

"Why would someone do this?"

Small and shaky, Jane's voice drifted down to him, and Rafe scrambled to his feet and took her in his arms. Holding her tight, he stroked her hair, cooed softly in her ear, "It'll be all right, baby."

"No, it won't," she said, peering up at him, her voice edging into hysterical. Tears stained her cheeks and reddened her eyes. "Someone obviously wants to hurt me. I just wish I knew why."

Scott stepped closer, his expression tight. "Let's talk inside."

Rafe led Jane, Scott and James into the kitchen where they all sat down.

"I think you should get Jane out of town for a while," Scott said. "It's obviously not safe for her here."

Jane's mouth twisted in irritation and Rafe knew she'd put up a fight. She wouldn't be chased from her home. And as much as the Neanderthal inside him wished to toss her over his shoulder and demand she do as she was told, he'd support her decision.

"It won't be safe for her anywhere until whomever is doing this is caught. Leaving town isn't going to help." The twisting of Jane's lips morphed into an appreciative smile instead.

"Then what do you suggest, Rafe?" the copper threw at him, slamming his hand on the table. "This wacko has escalated from graffiti to arson in a day, and I am no closer to figuring out who the fuck it is, where the fuck they are, or what they hope to achieve beyond scaring the crap out of Jane." He pushed himself back in his chair. "It's just me and one constable for the whole bloody town. We're not equipped for this."

"Settle down, son," James interjected, always the voice of reason. "Yelling and screaming won't help you figure this out any faster." Leaning back in his chair, he folded his arms over his beefy chest and stared at Jane, his gaze shrewd. Rafe wanted to shield her from those perceptive eyes, protect her from all of it, but he didn't know how. "Sweetheart, think hard," James said kindly. "Who would want to hurt you?"

Hands clenching into fists, Jane shook her head. "I don't know. I didn't have any enemies at work and as far as I know I don't have any enemies socially. I try to get along with everyone. In fact I make a point of getting along with everyone because the world is a shitty place and more people should try to get along and of course I have run-ins with people—who doesn't?—but nothing that warrants this sort of retaliation.

"And the only people I can think of who *might* have wanted to hurt me already did that when they stole all my money and flew off into the sunset together so unless Sleazebag Sam and Fake-Tits McGee are back in town, I honestly don't have the foggiest fucking clue who's doing this."

Resting his hand over her fist, Rafe squeezed gently until she relaxed her fingers and threaded them through his. Then he noted the look of shell-shock on the other men's faces.

Jane's verbal vomit bordered on legendary within the community, but not many people had ever experienced it first-hand. What Scott and James had just witnessed was pretty tame, comparatively speaking, but obviously more than they'd bargained for.

You never forget your first time....

"Sorry," she muttered, looking away as colour bloomed on her cheeks. "I can be overly wordy when I'm stressed. Or excited. Or hungry. Or, you know, awake."

Hating the embarrassment he saw etched across her face, Rafe hauled Jane into his lap, settled his arms around her waist and nuzzled her cheek.

"You've done nothing to be sorry for."

Jane turned her head to face him and gnawed at her lower lip. Worry bracketed her mouth and unshed tears glistened in her eyes, and Rafe knew she was barely holding it together. He knew because that was exactly how he felt, sitting in his kitchen, frightened for his family.

And there wasn't a bloody thing he could do about it.

After a beat of awkward silence, Scott cleared his throat. "Okay," he said, then looked at Rafe. "What about you?"

He shrugged. "What about me?"

"Come on, Bennett. You specialise in family law. Divorces and child custody disputes were your bread and butter. You have to have had some clients who weren't completely happy with your work. Is it possible someone's trying to hurt you by hurting Jane?"

A chill swept over Rafe's skin and he gritted his teeth against the sensation of dread coiling in his gut. Was it possible this was actually about him and not Jane?

Shit.

Chapter Sixteen

The thought someone might be after Rafe and not Jane had never even entered her head. It should have. He was a lawyer, and lawyers were never at the top of anyone's list of favourite people.

But even now, as they drove around Maroochydore on the hunt for a new family car, she couldn't think of why anyone would want to harm him.

Except maybe Patricia Leighton for what he'd said to her in the patisserie. But as bitchy and entitled as the woman was, even she wasn't arrogant enough to think she could get away with arson.

Jane frowned. Was Rafe the real target? He didn't seem to think he was, but he'd not dismissed the idea completely when Scott had brought it up.

"Not if keeping an open mind means keeping you and the baby safe," he'd said, as they'd sat around the kitchen table. He'd followed that with, "They must be staying somewhere in town. Think about it. Melville's Cross is twenty minutes off the highway and thirty minutes from the closest neighbouring town. If they were staying somewhere else they'd need a car. And this is a *small* town. Everyone notices when a new car drives down Main Street."

"Makes sense," Scott said. "We figured the only way they could be getting in and out undetected, is if they're on foot. But we've already checked with all the rental cottages, the boarding house, the bed and breakfast and anyone who lists their property on Airbnb, and no luck. No one has rented to anyone new in weeks."

Then Jane had suggested, "What if they're squatting?"

Scott and James had looked at each other then, and shared some sort of non-verbal communication between father and son. Jane had felt as if she were watching the twins. Charlie and Toby could have entire conversations with little more than a mouth twitch and a subtle shifting of their eyebrows.

"Would explain why we haven't seen any *new* cars," Scott had eventually said.

If someone was squatting in Melville's Cross, they'd have their pick of houses. Several of their more well-to-do citizens lived in the city during the week and only came home on the weekends. Others only came to town during the holidays, leaving their beautifully furnished houses, complete with million dollar views of the mountains, a fully stocked pantry and even occasionally their spare car, sitting vacant.

Just waiting for an opportunistic terrorist to take up residence.

The result of their conversation was to test their theory, hence why Rafe and Jane were spending their Sunday driving around the Sunshine Coast.

To see if anyone followed them.

Rafe had made his misgivings about the plan well and truly known when he'd said he'd much prefer locking her safely in their room and letting the police handle it. But Jane was determined not to live in fear. She'd already lost so much.

She wasn't losing her freedom too.

Scott promised not to let either of them out of his sight, just in case it was Rafe the mystery person was after, and not Jane. And while they were driving around, floating from one car dealership to the next, test-driving SUVs and keeping their eyes peeled for anyone suspicious, James was helping the young police constable back in Melville's Cross, checking out potential squats under the guise of performing fire safety checks.

"The car comes with six airbags, reverse driving camera plus front and rear climate control, heated seats—which admittedly is more of a luxury for the southern states—a spacious boot, and a ten inch touchscreen display."

Jane was so focussed on looking for something—anything—out of the ordinary, she'd almost forgotten the car sales guy was in the car with them.

Thankfully Rafe was on the ball. "Baby? Whaddaya think?"

Something in her brain clicked when he said the word "baby" and she remembered the other plan they'd made. Shoving aside her anxiety over what insanity their faceless foe would throw at them next, she focussed on the matter at hand.

It was time to bring her ditzy alter-ego out to play.

"So I can connect *any* smartphone to this, right?" she said, pointing at the touchscreen like her manicure was still wet. "I don't need a specific brand of phone? Because that would *totally* be a deal breaker for me."

Rafe made a choking sound then cleared his throat to hide his laughter.

"Yes, any recent make or model smartphone will work," the salesman assured her, somehow managing to make his voice sound both flirty and condescending at the same time, a trait Jane had thought, until now, unique only to the Chef de Cuisine.

Jane continued asking questions, gauging the salesman's answers against what she'd already researched, all while Rafe drove the SUV around the block and back to the dealership.

When he parked the car where the sales guy indicated and killed the engine, he stared at Jane, his amusement clear in his deep blue eyes. "Well?"

Without showing her face to the bloke in the back seat, she managed to flash her lover a grin and a wink. "I think...." The salesman leaned forward, a ready smile on his face. "It's about ten thousand dollars overpriced, considering the new model was released two weeks ago. I also think...."

Jane relaxed back into her old "bossy" self. The self-assured, ball-busting force of nature who fought for what she wanted, and won.

Hello me! I've missed you.

By the time she was done with the salesman, she'd reduced the overall price by seven grand, convinced him to throw in a fabric treatment for the seats for free, plus complimentary carwashes for twelve months.

An hour later, after negotiating paint colour—red, because Rafe drew the line at her suggestion of pink—and finalising the contracts, she was more than ready to go home.

"Poor bloke didn't know what hit him," Rafe murmured in her ear as he helped her into the passenger seat of his car. "Nicely done."

Before they left, Scott texted to let them know he'd seen

no one and nothing out of the ordinary, but he'd follow them home just the same.

Just in case.

Jane sat quietly, staring out the window at the passing scenery as they left the ocean views behind them and headed back up into the hinterlands. She was tired, and so was Rafe. Which was to be expected after the mayhem of the previous night.

After everyone had left The Forge, Rafe had taken her to bed. Her emotional exhaustion meant she'd quickly fallen into a restless sleep, but every little noise, every creak of timber, every whistle of wind had awoken her with a start, made her jump and grind her teeth against the helplessness burning a hole in her stomach.

And every time she woke up, there was Rafe, murmuring quietly in her ear that everything was all right, that he was there with her. Holding her, rocking her gently until she fell asleep again.

She looked at Rafe and watched him stifle a yawn.

"Do you want me to drive?" she said, knowing what his answer would be before she'd even asked the question.

"I'm good. We're only fifteen minutes from home now anyway."

Jane stared out the window again.

Why was this happening to them?

Yes, Rafe was a lawyer and yeah, sure, everyone hates lawyers, but he was a good man. He'd spent his life helping people, getting women and children out of abusive situations, helping single dads retain custody of their children when they'd been proven the more reliable parent.

He made sure siblings stayed together during custody disputes and worked so many pro bono cases he could probably declare himself a charity organisation.

Jane was proud of the work he did.

She was proud of *him*. Of Rafe.

He was her knight in shining Armani.

And as for her...? What could anyone possibly hope to gain by going after her? She'd already lost everything.

She glanced at Rafe, then down at her swollen belly. *Almost everything.*

"Are you feeling all right?" Sliding his hand over her thigh, he gave her a reassuring squeeze. The warmth of his palm, even through the denim of her jeans, calmed her lingering worries.

"I'm okay," she said. "I guess I thought...." She blew out a huff of breath, fanning the hair that had fallen over her forehead. "I guess I'd *hoped* we'd catch our mystery slut-shaming firebug today. Seen them, at the very least."

Rafe squeezed her thigh again. "I know. I'd hoped we would too. Maybe James and the constable found something while we were away. And hey, silver lining," he said, sliding his hand over her stomach. "We got our new family car. We can pick her up next week."

Layering her hands over his, Jane sent her lover a healthy dose of come-hither side-eye. "S*ooo* when we get home...."

"Yeah?" Rafe's mouth curled in a grin as they turned down Melville's Cross Road.

"I thought I might pamper your sexy arse with a bubble bath and a massage. And maybe a blowjob." She nodded. "Definitely a blowjob."

Rafe laughed then opened his mouth to speak, but a metallic glint by the side of the road caught her attention and she missed whatever it was he said.

Turning to look out the window, Jane's mouth fell open, poised to scream as horror and recognition flooded her with adrenaline and panic. Instinct kicked in, and in the few precious seconds before the plain white ute ploughed into them, she curled herself protectively around her baby.

Metal crunched and glass exploded. Wheels screeched and horns wailed.

Her seatbelt locked tight around her as the car was shunted sideways into oncoming traffic, and she flinched at the bang, bang, bang in the interior of the car.

An incessant ringing in her ears made her head ache and pain radiated through every inch of her body. Her face felt wet, the sickly stickiness of blood stuck her hair to her face and she tasted copper in her mouth.

Blurry masses of colour rushed around the car. Her inability to focus was annoying. Why couldn't she see? Where was she? And what was pushing against her?

Words filtered in and out of the chaos, their volume oscillating between the softest of whispers and incoherent screaming.

Wait, was that her? No. Who was that?

She swallowed hard against the sudden dryness in her throat.

"Don't move her."

"Watch her neck."

"She's pregnant."

"Baby, stay with me."

"Ra...?" Jane wasn't sure if she said the name out loud or if it was all in her head. She knew her mouth had moved because, like everything else, it hurt like hell. Breath wheezing in and out of her, she tried again to speak. She had to tell Rafe, she had to warn him.

"Ra...el...." A steel band tightened around her lungs, constricting their movement and any further words she might speak were lost in the noise.

"*Shhh*, baby. Everything's going to be okay."

Rafe sounded worried. Sad. Like he was crying. Rafe never cried. He was strong. The strongest man she knew. And if he was crying....

Oh God.

Her baby. *Their* baby.

No....

Eyes wide, a trickle of dread slid under her skin and she shivered. She was cold, shaking. Goosebumps broke out all over her body. Jane shook her head to clear the fog.

Bad move.

Everything shifted sideways, the fog thickened and the world faded to black.

Chapter Seventeen

"Mr Bennett, this really will go faster if you sit still."

As the ER nurse attempted yet again to bandage his wrist, Rafe's mind was a whirlwind of agony, the uncertainty of what was happening to Jane making his leg bounce at a near uncontrollable clip.

He couldn't "sit still" if his life depended on it.

"I need to be with my girlfriend. I need to know if—" He bit the words off. He couldn't say it.

He couldn't—wouldn't—contemplate the worst.

Blood.

There'd been so much blood.

After the crash, Rafe had staggered from the car and fallen to the ground, dazed and confused. A high pitched ringing had buzzed in his head like angry bees.

What the fuck happened?

Scott had been on him in an instant, his mobile phone plastered to his ear as he called for help.

He'd propped Rafe against the side of the car then gone to check on Jane and the other driver, then Rafe had heard his old friend curse and the click of handcuffs being snapped into place.

Struggling to his feet, he'd half climbed back into the driver seat where all his worst nightmares awaited him.

Jane's side of the car had borne the brunt of the collision. She was disoriented and pushed ineffectually at the slowly deflating airbags to her front and side.

Blood trickled down her temple and matted her hair in clumps, and on closer inspection he saw she had glass stuck in her forehead.

But that wasn't what sent a shiver down his spine.

No, that horrible feeling came when he slid his hand over her inner thigh and it came away slick with blood. Dark crimson and wet, it had been everywhere, had soaked through her jeans and into the seat, and he hadn't held back his cry of despair.

Blinded by tears and panic, he'd tried to unfasten Jane's seatbelt but it was jammed.

Or maybe it was him.

His hands had shook so violently he could barely grip the buckle, and the blood made them slip across the metal without purchase.

Scott had barked at him. "Don't touch her, wait for the doctor. Talk to her and keep her calm."

Something about that had made sense to him, reached his more logical side, even through the fog of his killer headache. So he'd reined in his anguish and done as ordered, with silent tears streaming down his cheeks.

Since the collision happened just outside Melville's Cross, Dr Chen and the other medical staff from the clinic arrived within minutes, as did the police constable, James and his RFS crew.

The firefighters had worked to free Jane and the other

driver from the cars while Dr Chen organised medical transport then tried her best to stabilise Jane.

When the EMTs arrived, they'd seen the handcuffs on the other driver. The junior ambo had scoffed and rolled his eyes. "Are those really necessary?" he'd asked, as though Scott was over-reacting to the fact the driver had just tried to kill them.

Scott got in the kid's face and drilled his finger into the idiot's chest. "She's our prime suspect in a series of crimes committed against Miss Melville," he snarled, pointing with his free hand at the gurney Jane was being strapped to. "Including arson, and now attempted murder. So, yes. They're necessary."

The kid looked like he might have pissed his pants. Scott continued barking orders at everyone while his constable re-directed traffic around the scene.

The drive to the hospital hadn't been fast enough for Rafe, and now he sat in the ER with a sprained wrist, a mild concussion and multiple contusions, while the love of his life was fuck knew where, all alone, and he couldn't go to her.

I'll never leave you again, Janie. I promise.

"I need to be with Jane," he said quietly, as the nurse helped him slide his arm into a sling.

Looking up from under her lashes, pity filled her gaze. "They were taking her for X-rays and an MRI, then an ultrasound."

"Do you know if she was awake?" She was unconscious when she'd gone into the ambulance.

The nurse shook her head. "I'm sorry, I don't. But I can ask. Wait here." Then she smiled kindly and disappeared through the slit in the curtains surrounding the bed he was sitting on.

"Wait here." Rafe snorted. Where the fuck did she think he was going to go?

When the nurse returned she had a doctor with her. He looked young and walked with a confidence that bordered on cocky. Rafe hoped he proved capable. He'd hate to have to punch a doctor.

"Rafe, my name is Dr Ellison. I'm the senior house officer on duty this afternoon." He picked up Rafe's file and flicked through the top few pages, then shone a penlight in his eyes and asked him an endless stream of questions until Rafe thought he might just punch the doctor on principle.

"Enough," Rafe snapped. "I want to see Jane. Where is she?"

The doctor clicked his pen and tucked it away in his coat pocket. "She's been admitted and we're running tests. I don't have any definitive information for you yet, except that she's been assigned a private room in the maternity ward."

Ice slid under Rafe's skin. The blood.

So much blood....

"When can I see her?"

"I'm not sure, but someone will come and get you as soon as we know more. In the meantime, there's quite a crowd gathering in the waiting room for you. We couldn't let them all in here, but we can bring in one or two, or if you prefer, you're well enough to sit out there with them while you wait. Choice is yours."

"I'll wait out there," Rafe said, and got to his feet, testing his balance before putting all of his weight down.

"That's fine," Dr Ellison said. "Just don't wander off, and let triage know if you start feeling dizzy again. Okay?"

"Sure."

Rafe exited the emergency ward into the waiting room

and almost collapsed in relief to see his family, and Mary Melville, filling half the room.

"Rafe!" Abby rushed forward and threw her arms around him, almost knocking him on his arse, then pulled back and apologised when he hissed in pain.

Twins, Charlie and Tobias—his only full-blood siblings —walked either side of him and ushered him into a seat. His father sat down on one side of him and Mary sat on the other. And all of them, every single one of them watched him like a ticking time bomb.

Waiting for him to explode.

"Is she— How is she?" Mary asked quietly. "They're not telling us anything."

Rafe took her hand in his and repeated what Dr Ellison had told him.

Then the dam broke.

The professional demeanour he prided himself on, that one that projected quiet confidence to his clients and colleagues alike, crumbled away, exposing his fear and his anguish and every other raw emotion he was too tired to name.

His shoulders slumped and his body shook, wracked by sobs. What if he lost her? What if after getting her back, what if after making her his again, he lost her to something a stupid as a car accident?

"I can't lose her again. I can't do this without her."

"Rafael," Mary said, her voice tight but stern. "She's made of tough stuff, our girl. She'll be all right. You'll see."

Rafe turned to the small woman beside him and enveloped her in his arms, clung to her as tightly as he clung to the hope he'd heard in her voice and prayed she was right.

A few minutes later, Scott walked in with a uniformed

police officer. Rafe couldn't hear the exchange between them but it looked official in capacity, and when Scott joined them a moment later, he explained, "The woman who caused the collision is Rachel Weis."

Rafe's hands clenched and he immediately regretted it, his sprained wrist throbbing in protest. "That's Sam Lyndon's girlfriend," he spat.

"Yes."

"Is Sam back too?" he demanded.

"Not according to Ms Weis. She confirmed they flew to Bali together and said they'd planned to travel via bus and small local airlines across Asia to India, then fly via commercial airline to Europe and disappear. But when she woke up after a night of celebratory drinking, Sam was gone. All he left behind was her passport, a non-refundable one-way ticket to Sydney, Australia and fifty bucks Aussie."

"He ran out on her too?" Oliver said with a snort. "What a charmer."

"How did she get from Sydney to Melville's Cross on fifty quid?" Mary asked.

Scott's features pinched and Rafe knew a look of disgust when he saw one. "She prostituted herself." Scott popped his jaw. "Gave men blowjobs for cash in bus stop bathrooms."

Right then Rafe knew Scott's disgust wasn't aimed at Rachel, but at Sam for putting her in that position. "Shit. Is she all right?"

"Physically? She has a broken nose and multiple contusions. Mentally? During the initial interview she sounded fine, but the police psychologist is speaking with her now so we'll have to wait and see."

"That fucking arsehole." Wolf.

"That poor girl." Mary.

Rafe's emotions flared again but swayed towards anger this time instead of despair. But losing his temper wouldn't get him the answers he needed, wouldn't get the job done.

He needed details. He needed information. He needed cool, calm facts.

Slowly, he let out the breath he'd been holding, centred himself.

Jane needed him. He couldn't afford to fall apart.

He stared at Scott. "Why come after Jane when it was Sam who screwed her over? What could she possibly hope to gain from any of this?"

Scott shook his head, as though he were having trouble believing it too. "She claimed Sam left her because of Jane."

Mary snorted. "Surely this girl doesn't think he actually *loved* Jane?" she said, one brow raised in a you-must-be-joking gesture.

"Nothing like that," Scott continued. "According to Ms Weis, before Jane came along, the most she and Sam had ever scored from one con was about fifteen thousand dollars. If I had to guess, I'd say Sam got greedy and didn't want to share. Figured now he'd hit the big time, he didn't need Rachel any more and ditched her."

"How the hell is that Janie's fault?" Oliver demanded.

"Ollie, I've been a cop for twenty years and I still don't understand half the things criminals do. She's been caught and she can't hurt Jane anymore. Focus on that."

"Mr Bennett?" A large man in dark blue scrubs called out from the ER doors.

Five deep voices answered at once. "Yes?"

"Ah... Mr *Rafael* Bennett? You can see Miss Melville now."

"Open your eyes, Janie," Rafe whispered. Clutching her hand in his, he pressed his lips to the backs of her fingers. "Please, please open your eyes."

Almost two days had passed since the crash.

When he and Mary had finally been allowed the see her, the doctors had rattled off a laundry list of injuries: three cracked ribs, a sprained ankle, two broken fingers, multiple contusions and head trauma.

Essentially, her brain had been knocked around inside her skull, was now seriously confused and needed time to rest, hence her state of unconsciousness.

"It's a common injury sustained in car accidents," they'd said. "We'll monitor her, of course, but there's nothing on her scans to indicate any permanent damage at this stage."

"How long until she wakes up?"

"It varies from one person to the next. I'm sorry I can't be more specific."

"And the blood?" he'd asked, barely daring to breathe.

"The ultrasound didn't show anything out of the ordinary. Foetus mobility looks good, heartbeats are strong," they'd said, flicking through Jane's file. "Sometimes bleeds, even heavy bleeds, just happen. Especially in multiple births."

"Multiple births?"

"Yes, Miss Melville is carrying twins. I'm sorry, I assumed you knew."

Twins.

Rafe no longer needed a blood test to know Jane's baby —babies—were his. Dr Chen had still confirmed it though when she'd stopped by to check on them. His DNA was a match.

He was going to be a father.

But, all the happy news in the world didn't change the fact Jane was still unconscious.

Doctors and nurses periodically came and went, taking her pulse, checking her vitals, changing her IV bag, whispering to each other just out of earshot as if sparing him the details of her condition was a kindness.

It wasn't.

Rafe was going crazy sitting there minute after minute, hour after hour, hoping, praying, begging, selling his soul to anyone who'd listen if only Jane would wake up.

To kill time, he'd tried pacing the room. It hadn't helped. He'd tried goading her into a fight, hoping she'd sit up and argue with him or tell him off or swear at him or something. But that hadn't worked either.

He scrubbed a hand over his face.

I'm so tired.

But he wouldn't leave her.

Couldn't leave her.

I promised.

His family had all stopped by at one time or another in the last couple of days, sometimes alone, sometimes in groups. They'd all tried to convince him to go home, to rest, to eat, shave, bathe.

In the end, Wolf and Abby had brought him clean clothes and a toiletries bag so he could shower and dress in Jane's ensuite bathroom.

He wasn't going anywhere.

Jane's family came and went too. Her father and brother had flown home from Sydney as soon as they'd heard about the crash. Richard had pored over her medical charts, argued with the attending doctor and demanded another ultrasound "just to be safe".

Her mother came during regular visiting hours and sat

quietly by Jane's side, stroking her hair and murmuring prayers, offering Rafe silent support and encouraging smiles.

But when her father visited, he just scowled.

He scowled at the doctors who told him there was nothing left to do but wait, he scowled at the nurses as they came and went, he even scowled at Jane, no doubt hoping as Rafe did that she'd wake up and scowl back. And he scowled at Rafe—at length—as if somehow this was all his fault.

Maybe it was. Maybe he should have fought harder for her, punched Sam in the face when he'd had the chance and stolen her away from him. Taken her to London or Paris or Melbourne or wherever she wanted to go and helped her live her dream.

Kept her safe.

"I was wrong."

Alec Melville's voice filled the room, those three softly spoken words somehow drowning out the endless loop of beeping and whirring emanating from the monitoring machines standing like sentinels on either side of the bed.

Rafe frowned at the older man, to where he'd suddenly appeared in the doorway with a plastic shopping bag clutched in his hand. "What?"

Entering the room, Alec closed the door behind him, then stood by the bed, his dark green eyes set on his daughter's pale face. "I was wrong," he repeated. "About you. About Jane." He sighed. "About everything."

The plastic bag rustled as Alec pulled something out of it and laid it by Jane's side, tucking it under her small hand. Rafe's heart sped up at the sight. A stack of papers bundled together with rubber bands, a British postage stamp sticking out from between the pages.

"My letters."

"Yes."

"When Jane asked Mary what had happened to them, she said she knew nothing about them." The air whooshed out of him as though someone had punched him in the gut.

She'd lied to them?

"She didn't," Alec said. "I intercepted them before Mary or Jane could see them. I even read a few. You write well. Eloquent, even." He sat heavily in the chair between the bed and the door and rubbed his knee. "She was so young, Rafael. Barely sixteen. I knew if she read your letters, she'd be lost to me."

"Lost to you?" Rafe scoffed, his hands curling into fists. "What the hell did you think I was going to do with her? Sell her into human trafficking?"

"I thought I was protecting her," Alec snapped. "But after you left—"

"You mean after you made me leave," Rafe snarled, his lip curling back from his teeth.

"Yes," Alec said, his voice flat, quiet. "When I made you leave... she changed. She grew cynical, hard. Cold. Her eyes lost their sparkle. When I made you leave, I broke my daughter's heart. I let this happen." He waved a hand at the bed. "I made her susceptible to men like Sam Lyndon, to men who would use her and discard her. By doing what I did, I made my little girl believe she was unworthy of love."

The older man scrubbed a hand over his face and Rafe saw the worry eating away at him, the lines bracketing his mouth and eyes, the permanent creases marring his brow. He looked as exhausted as Rafe felt.

"I didn't see it at the time, thought it was nothing more than a crush, that if we separated the two of you, she'd move on in time and start dating someone more appropriate, someone her own age." Sighing heavily, he shook his head. "But that didn't happen. She flitted from one relationship to another, a different boy every few months. She was so lost. The only time she was ever happy was when you were around, but by then the damage was done.

"She held herself apart, even from you, protected herself from any more hurt, and all because I'd made her think the man she loved didn't love her back." He took Jane's hand in his. "I'm so sorry, Janie. I only wanted to protect you."

Then he sat back in his chair and sighed. "I suppose you'd like an apology too," he said, but Rafe wasn't paying attention.

Jane was looking up at him, blinking slowly.

Her voice cracked as she whispered, "Rafe."

He was by her side in an instant, stroking her hair away from her face and pressing the softest of kisses to her cracked lips.

He looked at Alec. "Buzz the nurse." Then he grabbed the cup of water from the bedside table and held it to her lips. "Drink, baby. Just a little sip. That's my girl. That's my good girl."

A moment later, he and Alec were being shuffled to the side and out of the way as a stream of medical staff filed into the room and began checking monitors and taking Jane's vitals. Rafe blocked it all out. It was white noise as far as he was concerned, an annoying hum of sound easily forgotten if he focussed on something more important.

Someone more important.

Jane.

She was his focus, his centre, and even when the doctors finally spoke to him and Alec, assuring them Jane and the babies were going to be 100 percent okay, his gaze never left hers.

"Babies?" Jane said, and Rafe's smile grew broader. "Plural?"

Rafe returned to her side, threaded his fingers through hers. "Yes, plural. Twins."

Shifting so their joined hands rested on her baby bump, Jane grinned. "I told you this was your doing," she whispered, her voice still hoarse from lack of use.

Rafe returned her grin wholeheartedly. "Yes, you did."

Alec's face softened as he looked at his daughter. "I'm glad you're okay, sweetheart. I have to call Mary, let her know you're awake."

"Dad?" Jane reached out for her father. Alec returned to her side and took her hand in his. "I heard what you said," she said quietly.

"We can talk about it later. When you're feeling better."

She shook her head. "No. Now." She swallowed hard.

Rafe held the water cup to her lips. "Small sips, Janie."

She pushed the cup away. "Dad, I understand why you did what you did. And I know I was too young, we both were, but I would have waited until the end of time for this man."

Her father hung his head and nodded. "I know."

"And do you also know Rafe did nothing wrong that night? He held me, kissed me, told me he loved me, but he never crossed that line. You want to know what he said when I asked him why? Because he respected me too much to begin our life together with a crime."

Alec's gaze snapped to Rafe's, his shock evident in his wide-eyed stare. Rafe tilted his chin up and gripped Jane's hand tighter. He wasn't sure what she hoped to achieve with this conversation, but figured a united front was probably called for.

Jane mirrored his expression. "Now, I believe you owe Rafe an apology. A proper one."

Her father's expression softened and a smile tugged at one side of his mouth. "You are so much like your mother," he said, then turned to Rafe. "Which I guess explains why she loves a dull bastard like you."

"Dad!" Jane snapped, immediately coughing with the effort.

Alec held his hands up in surrender. "I'm sorry, Rafael. For the dull bastard comment, and for doubting your integrity," he added, his tone sincere. "My daughter is lucky to have a man like you in her life, and you're lucky to have her." He rested his hand on her shoulder. "I am proud of you, Jane, and all you've achieved over the years. And I'm sorry you ever doubted that." He took a breath. "Now, I really must call your mother," he said, and disappeared into the hallway.

Rafe helped Jane sit up, propping pillows behind her until she got annoyed at him and swatted him away.

"Stop making such a fuss," she said. "I'm fine."

He scowled at her, growled at her. "You almost died, Jane. You are most definitely not fine." Then he blinked slowly and hung his head, looked up at her from under his lashes. "Don't ever do that to me again, baby," he said, and no power in the world could've stopped his voice from cracking at that point. Sobs of relief and untold emotion wracked his body as the pain and the worry of the last two days were set loose. Burying his face in the crook of her neck, he said, "I don't know what I'd do without you."

"I'm not going anywhere, lawman." Jane's voice whispered over him, soothed him, and she stroked her hands over his head and neck, across his shoulders. Rubbed her cheek over his cropped hair.

"Ah... Rafe?"

"Yeah, baby?"

"Where's my hair?"

Rafe sniffed back his tears as a bubble of laughter rose inside him. He'd wondered how long it would take her to notice. Not long apparently. He fingered the much shorter strands of pale ginger hair framing her lovely face. "The firies cut a huge chunk out of your hair when they cut the seatbelt getting you out of the car. The nurses tried to even it up a bit but... I think a trip to the hairdresser might be in order when we get you out of here."

She felt around her head, her fingers pulling at her hair, testing its length and a stricken look overtook her pretty features. It was very short. "I've never had short hair before."

Rafe heard her unspoken question. "I think it looks sexy."

"Yeah?" Her voice said she wasn't so sure, but her mouth tipped up in one corner. "It doesn't make me look too much like my mum?"

"Are you saying your mum isn't sexy?" he teased.

Her eyebrows shot into her hairline. "Are you saying she is?"

He pretended to frown at her, the smart, funny, courageous love of his life. "I think you need to rest now. You're very tired."

"Oh my God." Jane chuckled, her emerald eyes wide and shining with humour. "You totally think my mum is sexy," she said, her voice scratchy.

He kissed a trail of feather-light kisses along the line of her jaw. "Not as sexy as you, beautiful."

Small hands scraped over his head and around his neck, urging him closer. "Rafe?"

He nibbled her earlobe. "Yes, Janie?"

"I love you," she sighed.

He leaned his forehead against hers. "I love you too."

"And Rafe?"

"Yeah, beautiful?"

"Will you marry me?" she whispered.

Rafe, careful of Jane's split lip, pressed his mouth to hers in the softest kiss he could manage, then smiled, happier than he'd ever been in his life. "I thought you'd never ask."

B risbane registry office, November, the best day of Jane Melville-Bennett's life.

"I, Elizabeth Jane, take you, Rafael Ulysses to be my lawfully wedded husband. I take you with all your faults and strengths, and will stand by your side through both success and failure. I will help you when you need help and I will comfort you when you need comfort. I will honour the trust you have placed in me," Jane repeated the vows Rafe had said to her only moments earlier. "I love you and cherish you, and choose to spend my life with you and no other."

She hiccoughed a laugh as her husband reached out and gently swiped her tears away with the pad of his thumb.

It had been almost two months since Jane had been released from hospital, her injuries had all but mended, and life had slowly gotten back to normal.

During the week she continued working at Straight to

the Hips, testing new recipes for her cook book on the unsuspecting public, plus Street Sweets Mobile Patisserie had officially launched. And thanks to a recent article and glowing review in Foodies Weekly magazine, the business was attracting a steady stream of weekend bookings, catering mostly to small weddings in out-of-the-way venues.

She and Rafe had bought their own place in Melville's Cross, on the opposite side of town from her parents' house —a private cottage in dire need of renovating but with magnificent views of the mountains and enough room for a nursery. Which they were going to need in approximately three months time.

But even with their crazy life, filled with home renovations and a new business and Rafe's legal office open to the public, they'd fallen into a comfortable routine. One that entailed ripping each other's clothes off and screwing each other's brains out at every given opportunity, as though they were trying to make up for lost time.

Sixteen years of it.

And Jane had finally gotten to read Rafe's letters.

Lines like *"Today's sunset reminds me of you, the bright red and orange clouds undulating across the sky make me think of the day we went swimming at the creek and your hair fanned out around you as you floated on the surface of the water"* and *"...went on a day trip to Ireland today. My heart ached for you and the sight of your beautiful eyes, as emerald and as lush as the rolling hills I saw all around me. I miss you so much, Janie. I love you so much. We'll be together soon. I promise"* had cracked open her heart and she'd sobbed uncontrollably.

She'd been ashamed to remember how she'd felt when he'd left her, then despaired at the time they'd lost because of her stubbornness and fear. Until Rafe had wiped her tears away and slid his hand over her belly, had felt the little lives inside her kick for the first time and reminded her they had the rest of their lives to be together. That their time apart had allowed them to grow, to date and love other people, and to realise they would always come back to one another.

Always.

Now she stood in front her loved ones, wearing a white cotton maternity dress her mother had embroidered with pale pink roses, getting married to the love of her life.

It seemed her perfect proposal wasn't Rafe asking her to marry him, but the other way around.

Jane didn't think it possible to be any happier than she was in that moment. Not without exploding into a million excitable pieces.

Of course, the exploding sensation could have been due to the copious amounts of water she'd drunk prior to the ceremony. Mother Nature had chosen her wedding day of all days to throw a tantrum and crank up the Queensland heat and humidity.

Her wedding was being held on the hottest November day on record in ninety-seven years. Also, being six months pregnant with twins, her babies and bladder were locked in an endless cage fight for dominance.

And her bladder was currently winning.

The marriage celebrant smiled indulgently. "Do you have the rings?" Oliver, who was acting as Rafe's best man, reached around his older brother and placed two matching loops of gold in the celebrant's slender hand. "Rafael, please place the ring on Jane's finger and repeat after me."

Rafe parroted the celebrant's words then slid the ring home.

"Jane, please place the ring—"

"I got this, babe," she said, and ignoring the snickering coming from their families, she quickly repeated what Rafe had said then slid the ring on his finger.

Rafe's brow pulled down as he stared at her, undoubtedly trying to figure out why she was rushing.

Jane pursed her lips together and tried not to squirm, but when Rafe's frown deepened she relented, whispering, "Pregnant lady, remember? I need to pee."

Oliver burst out laughing, Abby, acting as her maid of honour, got a fit of the giggles, and the celebrant blushed. Rafe cupped her face in his big warm hands, then grinned unrepentantly at the celebrant until the poor woman shook her head, threw her hands in the air and said, "You may kiss the bride."

And he did.

Jane's toes curled in her shoes as Rafe kissed her slowly, deliberately and without any room for doubt that he loved her.

And always would.

The End

I hope you enjoyed Jane and Rafe in

THIS TIME AROUND

Please consider sharing the love by leaving a review for
other readers to find. It doesn't need to be very long, and
every review is greatly appreciated.

Want something sexy yet sweet?
Check out Jennie Kew's steamy romance series,
The Brisbane Bachelors Series.

Want something short and not-so-sweet?
Check out Jennie Kew's short erotic stories,
The Q Collection.

For more information about
The Bennett's Bastards Series visit
www.jenniekew.com

More from Jennie Kew

The Bennett's Bastards Series
Third Time Lucky

This Time Around

His Own Heaven

The Viking Blues (coming 2021)

Size Doesn't Matter (TBA)

The Brisbane Bachelors Series
Revenge and Redemption

Sacrifice and Seduction

Torment and Temptation (TBA)

Audiobooks
Revenge and Redemption

The Q Collection
No Rest For The Wicked

I Saw, I Conquered, I Came

Pushing Rope

Dirty Laundry

Santa Claus Is Coming

Between A Rock And A Hard Place

Tying The Knot (TBA)

The Q Collected

Dirty: 3 Short Contemporary Stories

Grind: 3 Short Paranormal Stories

The Whole Shebang (TBA)

Acknowledgements

To my family for all their encouragement, their love and understanding, thank you for being you and for putting up with me being me, especially when deadlines are involved.

A special thank you to my crit partners, my cheer squad, my sisters-in-arms, Bec McMaster and Kylie Griffin. You always challenge me to be a better writer and I really couldn't do this without you. Thank you for keeping me sane...*ish*.

To my editor, Kristin Scearce, who accepts my weird writing style and quirky humour as canon and is still willing to work with me, you rock!

And finally to my readers, thank you for taking this journey with me, and for allowing me to share with you all the people and places who occupy my head and my heart. I hope you enjoy reading about them as much as I enjoy writing about them.

Meet the Author

Jennie has always enjoyed reading but is a relative late-comer to writing. She never had aspirations of becoming a published author until a dance with death made her ask herself what she really wanted out of life, and she's been writing ever since.

When not sitting in front of her computer, Jennie can usually be found reading a book, watching a movie or building stuff out of Lego.

She lives in regional New South Wales, a stone's throw from Australia's capital, Canberra, with her husband, her husband's magnificent beard, a teenage giant and their feline overlords, Max and Tallulah.

www.jenniekew.com

Glossary

As all of my books are set in Australia and use a lot of Australian terms and slang, I've created this guide for my readers to keep you on track when you come across any Aussie-isms in my books.

A bit of all right: If someone is 'a bit of all right' they're considered to be very attractive.

Ambo: Short for ambulance, the term has come to mean anyone associated with any of the public or private ambulance services, their drivers and paramedics.

Arse: Aussie spelling of ass, aka buttocks, bottom, booty and bum.

Arvo and *Sarvo*: Afternoon and 'this afternoon'.

Copper: On occasion, Australians will actually lengthen words or use them in their original format. Cops (i.e. The police) was originally 'copper'.

Fashion Rag/Local Rag: Fashion magazine, any locally produced magazines or newspapers.

Fierie/s: Firefighter/s.

Fuck-knuckle: An idiot.

G'day: Pronounced 'gidday', this official Australian (and Kiwi) greeting is a contraction of the words 'good' and 'day'.

Kiwi: Pronounced 'kee-wee', A person from Middle Earth (New Zealand).

Larrikin: An unruly, boisterous but generally good natured person, usually male.

Mate: Unlike paranormal or sci-fi erotic romances where your 'mate' is the person you're fated to be with for the rest of your life, in Australian culture 'mate' could mean anyone from your best friend to some random bloke you just met.

Pav: Pavlova, a dessert made from baked meringue, topped with cream and fresh fruit, particularly popular around Christmas. We nicked it from the Kiwis.

Phwoar: An estimation of the sound one makes when a bit of all right enters your vicinity. See also, 'panting' and 'drooling'.

RFS: Rural Fire Service.

Sanga: Sandwich.

She'll be right, mate: Usually given as a response when someone is offering aid of some kind, it means 'Everything will be fine but thanks for asking'.

Togs: A swimsuit.

Tradie: Any tradesman.

Uni: Pronounced 'you-nee', University aka College.

Yeah, nah and *Nah, yeah*: Another instance where Australians have made something sound more complicated than it needs to be, is 'Yeah, nah' and 'Nah, yeah'. Whichever word the phrase ends on, is the affirmative answer, therefore 'Yeah, nah' means 'No' and 'Nah, yeah' means 'Yes'.